THE TROUBLE IN TENERIFE

A John Dunn Mystery

Marilyn Joyce Lafferty Sietsema

CONTENTS

Foreword

A lover of mystery stories and of traveling to romantic places, Marilyn Sietsema created this novel to express and commemorate that love. The Canary Islands were one of Marilyn's favorite destinations and many of her cherished sceneries are described here in print. The characters in the story have characteristics of family and friends, and many of you who knew Marilyn may recognize yourself. We believe Marilyn wrote this sometime in the mid-1980s though the exact date it was completed is unknown. Marilyn never attempted to publish this during her life. The manuscript was discovered after her death and we have published it for your reading pleasure.

Robert, David, and William Sietsema

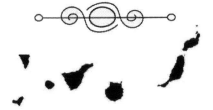

CHAPTER I: The Meeting

John Dunn stepped from a cab into the misty January rain and zigzagged his way through New York's crowded Kennedy International Airport. His flight was due to leave at 7:00 P.M., and as he glanced quickly at his watch, he determined that he had at least 30 minutes before his flight was due to depart. This was not exactly ample time, but if the system did not fail him, he would have just enough time to check his luggage, declare his camera equipment with customs, and buy the flight insurance his wife felt would be necessary to prevent any untoward air transportation accident. John had never been able to convince Irene that this was a waste of money and a tribute to her superstitious nature. As he knew, her reply to his comments about this would always be, "It must work dear, you have never had an accident." If it gave her peace of mind, it was probably worth the cost.

He arrived at the check-in counter to discover a long line of irritated passengers, bundled up to their chins against the outside cold and damp, unable to remove the extra scarves and gloves because of hands already claimed by assorted luggage and umbrellas. He was grateful to his company for letting him travel first class. Although it was more costly, it meant he would arrive at his destination better able to effectively solve the problems his company's overseas operations had generated.

He hurried to the special first-class desk, checked his luggage, and went directly to the Customs Office. There was no line here, but the door labeled 'U.S. Customs', although invitingly open, was devoid of personnel to process his declaration. He impatiently rang the bell on the counter and was eventually rewarded by the return of the Customs Officer from his coffee break.

"Can I help you sir?"

"Yes, I'd like to declare my camera equipment before catching my flight to Madrid."

"We can do that in a few minutes. Just fill out these forms please."

John hurriedly filled out the forms he had been given, recorded the serial numbers of his 35 mm camera and the assorted lenses and ancillary equipment he always carried with him. The idea was that by declaring these items prior to departure, he would not be hassled about paying duty on them when he returned.

"Thank you," said John as he handed the officer the completed forms. He was given a receipt which he carefully tucked into his wallet.

"Have a nice trip," the customs officer replied.

Having disposed of this Customs task, he returned to the main waiting area and purchased the necessary insurance just as his flight was called. He arrived at his first-class seat, removed his lightweight gabardine Burberry, and handed it to the stewardess to hang in the front closet. His camera bag was placed beneath the seat and, as he lowered himself into the seat, he gave an almost imperceptible sigh of relief. There was always a feeling of accomplishment for John on these overseas trips when he was finally settled in his seat. The preparations for these flights were always fraught with the tensions of concentrated activity. He had to make sure he had everything with him that he would need; not only certain test equipment, formulas, manuals, and the like, but also the personal items he depended on for his day-to-day routine. To leave behind important machine parts could cause countless delays in completing the job he had to do plus unnecessary added expense. To forget personal items was just irritating.

The stewardess had already decided that Mr. Dunn, trim, well dressed, and slightly grey at the temples, was probably the vice president of some well-known Fortune 500 company and showed him the respect due him by asking if he would like to order a drink to be served as soon as the flight departed. She frequently played the game of guessing the status or occupation of the passengers she served. She had her own rule of never asking questions as this would be an intrusion into a stranger's privacy, but sometimes the travelers themselves gave her the answers to her mental questions. When her guesses proved correct, she was always delighted. She was sometimes greatly amused when her suppositions were completely incorrect. With an eye to relaxing completely and making the best of a tedious eight-hour flight, John gratefully accepted the stewardess' offer of a drink.

Immediately the flight rose gracefully into the air, the stewardess brought him his Scotch-on-the-rocks. Subsequently, she took the order of the heavy set, blonde man who had positioned himself in the seat next to John. He had arrived just before the plane door was secured. This man, in his late thirties, appeared to be somewhat younger than John. He gave the appearance of being a typical American businessman departing for the European Continent to make important decisions for his company. His tousled, somewhat disoriented countenance led John to think that he must have a lot on his mind. He smiled detachedly at John, then, as if remembering his manners, introduced himself as Wayne Morrison. He seated and secured himself and immediately opened his brief case when the plane was airborne. After sorting through the dog-eared papers contained in his case, Wayne turned to John and asked, "You stopping in Lisbon?"

"No", was John's reply. "I'm going on to Madrid, and from there I will fly to the Canary Islands. Tenerife to be exact."

"You in sales?" Wayne continued.

John explained that he was basically an engineer and served as a trouble shooter for Amco Manufacturing. It was his job to help plants which were having production problems. He was on call twenty-four hours a day. It was not unusual for him to receive a call in the middle of the night. These night calls were, more often than not, from production managers in foreign countries in different time zones. Managers with serious production line problems were frequently so panic stricken that they were not concerned about whether the person they were calling was in bed. When John received a call, it was his custom to pack his bag immediately, make plane reservations for the following day, and then promptly return to bed. He was lucky that it was easy for him to go back to sleep after being awakened in the middle of the night.

Wayne was aware that Amco was a large conglomerate in the business of manufacturing a variety of household aids such as soaps, dish washing detergents, and toothpaste, as well as cake mixes, packaged snacks, and candies. It was a well-known fact that Amco had entered the international field and that during the past few years had been making spectacular inroads into European markets. Of course, because of the government regulations of many of the countries on the continent, Amco had found it necessary to do most of the manufacturing right in the country where the goods were to be marketed. Amco was not opposed to this and could fully understand why some countries objected to purchasing the items their citizens required directly from the United States. They didn't want their balance of trade tipped against them and, in addition, they were working toward a more fully employed population of their own.

Personally, John felt that completely free international trade would benefit all countries. Price and demand would identify the nature of products to be manufactured. However, even John's own country had too many special interest groups to permit this.

Wayne indicated that he also was interested in international business. His position seemed less readily definable. He told John that he had his own small import business. Apparently, Wayne would scout the continent for items which would appeal to Americans, develop a quantity purchase price at the point of origin, and then contract with well-known American department stores, specialty shop suppliers, and catalog companies to buy portions of the goods for resale to their own customers. He mentioned that his clients included two posh mail-order houses. Their needs required not only that he find unique, impressive items, but that he be able to supply an unlimited number of these items if they proved popular. If the items didn't sell well, Wayne had to be willing to receive payment only for those that were sold, and to find another market if he was left with an overstock.

Wayne specifically mentioned that he was currently on a buying jaunt to Madrid, and that this trip might take him south to Toledo or Seville, but no further. He expected to be returning to the States in somewhat under a week's time.

On a flight as long as this one, from New York to Lisbon and then to Madrid, it was quite usual for passengers to establish temporary friendships, if for no other reason than to alleviate the inevitable boredom that resulted from almost eight hours of sitting in the confines of an airplane. Thus it was that Dunn and Morrison became close companions. After the meal was served, with the usual after dinner drinks, their companionship extended to discussions of personal interests.

John described his wife. Although he was hardly away from home, it was apparent that he already missed her. Dr. Irene Dunn was director of the Poison Control Center in Manhattan. She supervised a staff of persons who accumulated pertinent information on just about any substance that humans could possibly ingest. This information was carefully cataloged for quick access in emergencies. Irene really liked her job, feeling that this was an area where she could help others.

Sometimes her job also included night duty, as everyone in the Center took their turn at being on call one evening every other week. For this service she could have a day off, which was helpful in attending to household, financial, medical, and dental chores, which were impossible to do on weekends.

John and Irene lived in an apartment in Manhattan as close to Irene's work as possible. Living in New York, they didn't own a car as parking and vandalism made it unfeasible. Also New York public transportation was quite good, and they could rent a car when they felt the need to escape from the city.

Wayne, as it turned out, was not married but planned eventually to settle down with a young lady who interested him; that is, if she agreed. He mentioned that he had a small, rented apartment in Manhattan but described its location in a rather nebulous fashion.

At about 11:00 P.M. the pert blonde stewardess came by to distribute nightcaps and the conversation turned to the merits of brandy versus a good Portuguese wine. Soon the lights in the plane were dimmed, pillows and blankets were distributed, and both men slipped into, if not a deep sleep, at least a relaxing light one.

At 5:30 the next morning it was announced that the plane would be landing in 45 minutes in Lisbon and would remain at the Portela de Sacazem for one-half hour before departing for Madrid. There would be no time for passengers who were continuing on to disembark.

As the 747 lifted off for Madrid again, a remarkable view of the Portuguese countryside could be seen from the plane window. In the rising sunlight, the fields below were bright glowing tan with deep green borders, each neatly partitioned into checkerboard dimensions. An occasional red tiled roof, rimmed by cream-colored walls, stood at the edge of a field.

John was happy that this trip was nearly over. By this afternoon he would be settled at his hotel in Santa Cruz de Tenerife, ready to begin work the following Monday; ready to solve the problems of local manufacturing. He noticed with surprise that Wayne had been quiet and thoughtful, maybe even somewhat distant since their departure from Lisbon. He had seemed so cheerful during breakfast. It isn't unusual for flight friendships to terminate abruptly when a plane lands, but he had enjoyed Wayne's company and conversation, and they seemed to have experienced such a feeling of camaraderie that he had somehow thought he might see him again.

John made a final overture by mentioning that he planned to exchange his American money for Spanish pesetas and then shop the stores at the Barajas Airport in Madrid while awaiting his flight to Tenerife. Wayne replied that this was an excellent idea and that he would join John if he didn't mind. He wouldn't be checking into his hotel, the Palacio Royale, until the afternoon anyway. Wayne had to pick up his luggage, so it was agreed that John would go at once to the currency exchange line and meet Wayne there after they had passed through passport control and customs.

The currency exchange window had a moderately long line, as was usually the case just following the landing of an international flight. It took about 20 minutes to complete the exchange transaction, and then John looked around for his friend. His heavy-set figure was not in evidence, so John wandered downstairs toward the luggage claim section. Wayne was not there. John asked the claims guard if a Mr. Morrison had picked up his baggage. John's halting Spanish was in no way helpful, but he thought he interpreted the guard as indicating that all luggage had been picked up from his flight. It was probably a misunderstanding. Wayne was most likely waiting for him upstairs near the shops.

He hurried in that direction but to no avail. He quickly made a cursory examination of the interior of each shop and then returned to first the currency exchange area and then the baggage claim section. By this time, the international section of the airport was fairly well cleared. Incredible, but Wayne seemed to have disappeared. "Ah well," thought John, "perhaps he changed his mind, or had met a friend." After making a leisurely examination of the shops, John retired to the coffee shop to await the arrival of his flight for Tenerife.

Marilyn Joyce Lafferty Sietsema

CHAPTER II: The Arrival

The landing at Tenerife was always a thrill.

Immediately after the plane departed from Madrid, it headed southwest and arrived back over the Atlantic Ocean. After about an hour and a half, a bit of land appeared quite suddenly in the distance. As the speck grew larger, it was apparent that it was comprised primarily of solid, dark brown rock. Approaching, the plane flew between solid rock cliffs and mountain tops. With sudden, breathtaking swiftness, the plane nosed down, as if bent on plowing directly into the ground. Just as John began to fear that this might actually happen, the plane leveled out and landed without incident at the Aeropuerto De Los Rodeos in Tenerife. This airport was but a miniature version of the Barajas airport in Madrid.

As John disembarked, he recognized the smiling faces of his friends. Antonio Sedena, official owner of the Amco subsidiary in the Canary Islands. His brother Guillermo, second in command, and the two secretaries, Rosa Ortuno and Alberina Venero, were also there to properly greet the newcomer. It was the custom in Tenerife to make a pleasant event of anything as important as a friend's arrival. John rather liked this custom. It made him feel welcome and made the hard work he would be engaged in the next few weeks more palatable. He greeted all his friends with warm hugs, and there was the usual happy exchange of inquiries as to the welfare of each other's families. Antonio and Guillermo had large families of seven and eight children respectively, so there was much to talk about.

Antonio told John, "You are looking good. How is Irene? My wife said to ask you when you are going to bring her to see us."

"She's fine. I have been getting the same question from her. I have told her so many times how beautiful it is here that she is anxious to see for herself. Perhaps next time I come to the Islands, I can plan ahead, and she can arrange to take a vacation from her job."

Guillermo chimed in, "I am really glad you could come and give us some help. I apologize for requesting your help on such short notice, but we desperately need your technical advice. Getting started with these wafer bars has provided us with one problem after another. We ordered the machinery exactly to specifications and followed the formulas precisely, and yet we are still having difficulties."

"I'm sure we can straighten things out," returned John.

"It's not unusual to have many frustrating little things go wrong when you are starting up a line. These things tend to iron themselves out in time. I shall probably be able to solve many of the problems fairly quickly, as I have worked with these machines before and understand their idiosyncrasies. Sometimes several adjustments must be made on the machinery, other times the formula needs to be revised."

"Why is this?"

"Well, the raw materials that are available here may be different than the raw materials we have been used to working with. Take flour for instance. Wheat grown in different parts of the world can produce flour with very different characteristics. One variety may produce flour with a high gluten content, whereas another variety may contain much less gluten. Therefore, preparing baked products using these different flours may require different amounts of water, sugar, or even different baking temperatures and times. It can become very complex, and the problem may require carefully controlled research to select optimum time, temperature, and amounts of other ingredients. It is the same with some of the other components that go into wafer bars. Don't worry though. We will get things straightened out." Soon they had claimed John's luggage and distributed themselves between two Peugeots belonging to the company.

The airport was located as high up in the foothills as feasible. This meant that it was several miles from Santa Cruz de Tenerife, the main town on the island, located on the coast. As the cars sped along toward the factory, John glanced from time to time at the passing countryside. Here and there were the rough stone cottages constructed without the benefit of mortar. So firmly put together were these houses, that they had served the inhabitants and their ancestors for centuries and would probably continue to outlast several more generations.

The Canary Islands had always fascinated John. On a previous visit, he had made it a point to learn something about their history and geography. The islands are part of an archipelago off the western coast of Africa, made up of thirteen islands of volcanic origin. Only seven are inhabited by any great number of people. The largest island is Tenerife.

The islands are divided into two provinces under Spanish jurisdiction. The province of Santa Cruz de Tenerife consists of the islands of Tenerife, La Palma, Gomera and Hierro. The province of Las Palmas de Gran Canaria includes Gran Canaria, Fuerteventura, Lanzarote, and all the remaining smaller, sparsely populated islands.

The original inhabitants of the islands, and especially Tenerife, are called Guanches, and their exact origin remains a mystery. The fact that many of them are blonde with blue eyes led to the theory that early Vikings may have settled there. Others claim that the Guanche language suggests deviation from a language common to the Mediterranean area during the Stone Age. Still others feel that the language of the original Guanches is somewhat related to Egyptian. Given the proximity of the islands to the coast of Africa (the closest island, Fuerteventura, being but 60 miles away), it was easy to believe that the Guanches may have originated there. It is known that isolated populations tend to inbreed and develop according to the limited genes of that population. It is possible therefore, that a blue eyed, blonde couple, outcast from the African continent could have settled in Tenerife and expanded, in time, to populate the island.

Carbon 14 dating of bone artifacts belonging to these early inhabitants suggests that they probably took up life on the islands towards the end of the third century A.D. All that is known about the Guanches comes from reports made by early travelers to the islands, beginning shortly before the 14th century. These travelers reported that at that time, the Guanches did not know the use of the wheel, had not learned to build boats, and that only slight contact was made between the closest islands, by swimming back and forth with inflated pig bladders and goat skins.

Reports are that the Guanches were troglodytes, living mainly in natural caves or in abodes hollowed out of the slopes of the mountains. In some instances, however, there remain examples of Guanche buildings constructed of stones carefully fitted together. Their dwellings were usually situated in the mountains and hills, as this rough and rocky terrain protected them from invaders. And many invaders there were.

The Canary Islands were often written about by ancient historians and were included in ancient myths. For Homer, the Canary Islands were known as the Elysian Fields. For Hesiod, they were the "Islands of the Gorgons". Plato considered the Islands to be the remains of the lost Atlantis. Plutarch told of a sailor who passed through the Pillars of Hercules (Gibraltar) and stopped at the Fortunate (Canary) Islands. It has been theorized by some, that the Islands got their present name because of the strange looking wild dogs that once roamed the Islands. The Roman word for dog is canis, hence the name Dog or Canary Islands. It is certainly true that the Islands abound with funny looking dogs with long, pointed snouts and ears. Partly it was the mysterious nature of the Islands that made them so intriguing to John. He fully intended to spend any free time he could muster exploring.

Today being Saturday, John felt sure he could find some time Sunday to begin his exploration. Although he would be loath to admit it, he was as eager to satisfy his curiosity about the Islands as he was to solve the production problems which would soon confront him. Both were a challenge and a chance to learn. Continued learning is a driving force behind most intelligent humans, and John was no exception. Besides, the breathtaking and novel scenery of the Island would give him a chance to exercise his photographic skills, another of his spare time interests.

As the cars reached the city of Santa Cruz, John recognized the Zona Industrial with its many petroleum storage tanks, so out of keeping with the rest of beautiful Santa Cruz. Soon they turned into the Avenida de los Reyes Catolicos, drove past the Plaza de Cominicans and finally angled into Avenida General Franco. When they reached the factory, they were greeted by the remainder of the office force. Again, the warm, cheerful welcomes made John feel at home. Antonio and Guillermo then spent some time in closed session with John discussing the problems of production. It wasn't until nearly six o'clock in the afternoon that Antonio suggested that John might like to check into his hotel. Plans were made for him to have dinner with them at 10 o'clock at the Yacht Club.

Guillermo drove John and his luggage to the Hotel Mencey. This was his favorite place to stay and someday he planned to bring his wife here for a second honeymoon. The atmosphere reminded him of the Charles Boyer movies he had seen on television. The original ceiling fans still wafted their cooling breezes down on those in the main lounge. The tropical garden in the center atrium was the perfect backdrop for the cool cloisters, paved in tiles, which surrounded it. Here one could lounge in complete peace and tranquility or move to the main lobby and "people watch" as travelers from all over the world checked in. It was common practice for the elderly ladies and gentlemen, who were more or less permanent residents, to sit by the check-in desk and attempt to guess the nationality of each entrant from their carriage and mannerisms.

After checking in at the desk, John was led to the ancient elevators, taken squeakily to the sixth floor, and then to a room overlooking a garden. The room was antiquated by American standards. It contained the ubiquitous narrow twin beds one expects to find in European style hotels and a white-tiled bathroom with an old-fashioned tub. There were heavy, slatted, wooden blinds affixed to the outside of each window. These could be cranked up or down and left closed or opened according to one's whim. These shades provided a method for dimming the room properly for an afternoon siesta. Neither heating nor air conditioning is required on Tenerife as the temperature usually remains between sixty and eighty-five degrees Fahrenheit year round.

With ease John lifted one suitcase to the luggage rack, unlocked it, and removed clean underwear, casual trousers, and a sport shirt. A leisurely shower, urged from the cantankerous plumbing, refreshed him, and he decided that the short nap he had planned could be dispensed with. He was eager to see more of Santa Cruz. He quickly dressed and headed downstairs for a look at the hotel and gardens.

He reflected that this hotel always had singular sounds not heard in other hotels. For one thing, the Mencey was very old. He guessed it had existed, with few changes, since the early nineteen-hundreds. Without heavy insulation and carpeting, sounds from all areas of the hotel blended in a sort of orchestrated harmony. The soft clanking of cutlery and dishes could be heard from the main floor dining room where tables were being set for the dinners to be served several hours later. The music of practicing musicians drifted up from the basement, where a small cabaret would open later. From the lobby came the soft buzz of people talking; luggage being scraped over the tile floors; cash register drawers opening, closing, and ringing up sales; and, in the background, always the squeaking and grinding of the overworked elevators.

Along with the sounds came delightful odors; the fresh sea breeze and the smell of blooming plants mixed with the appetite enticing roast lamb and fresh-from-the-oven rolls, all interlaced with occasional wafts of exotic perfumes from passing ladies. These smells were effectively transported and dispersed to every corner of the first floor by the softly whining ceiling fans. With such an atmosphere, who would opt to stay in one of the newer, plastic hotels?

John wandered into the outdoor garden and admired the many brilliant shades of Bougainvillea rambling over the stucco walls and fences. Tropical trees and greenery served as a backdrop. He ambled through the garden gate out onto the sidewalk which stretched up the hills immediately in back of the hotel. The sidewalk was hedged on one side by the high stucco fence walls of every home it passed, and on the other by a narrow brick road. Taxis lined the curb. Their drivers busily polished them and talked with each other animatedly. The drivers interrupted their polishing and talking briefly as John approached, until they were certain he was a stroller and not a potential passenger. Then they continued with their chatter.

As he strolled up the steep sidewalk, he admired the poinsettias growing as heavy vine-like trees, over, or in front of, every stucco fence. The fences were eight to ten feet high and most had small, sharp, chunks of broken glass imbedded in their top surfaces. John remembered that the purpose of this glass was to prevent cats from staging howling fence-top battles during the night hours when the homeowners were trying to sleep. It also occurred to John that these fences would certainly be effective crime preventers.

John's stroll led him past many old houses with their typical intricately carved, lace-like, wooden balconies. In the distance, higher up the hills, could be seen goats grazing in the backyards of the shacks and shanties of the disadvantaged population of Santa Cruz. This was a typical example of how affluence and poverty existed in close proximity in the Canary Islands.

Returning to the hotel, he changed into more formal attire for dinner and went downstairs. He waited at the entrance to the hotel for Guillermo to pick him up at 9:30. As he waited, he glanced down the sidewalk to the far entrance of the hotel and saw, or thought he saw, Wayne Morrison emerge and stroll quickly down the street and around the corner. There was not time to hail him as Guillermo arrived just at that moment.

Dinner was pleasant and John was pleased to have the opportunity to visit with the wives of Antonio and Guillermo. They described the many antics of their respective offspring. John enjoyed being around children himself, so he could truly laugh at the tales they told. He had always hoped that Irene and he would have some children of their own, but apparently this was not going to happen. After all, they had been married for over 15 years.

The food and wine were delicious and when the dining was over all the people at the club gathered into groups and formed circles, arm in arm. They sang joyous and sad songs while swinging from side to side, in time with the music. "So much better than the custom of sitting at home watching TV," thought John to himself. The party wound down by 1:30 A.M. and the couples and families gradually left for home.

John felt pleasantly drowsy and ready for sleep when Guillermo dropped him off in front of the hotel. Even the somewhat lumpy mattress and the noise from celebrants in the garden and night owls in the surrounding town couldn't keep him awake. However, just before drifting off, or perhaps it was as he was drifting off, his subconscious mind pulled the thought of Wayne from its depths, forcing him to cogitate, if briefly, on the unexplained disappearance and the possible reappearance of his recent acquaintance. He wasn't quite sure whether he had really seen Wayne or if it was only someone resembling him.

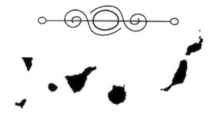

CHAPTER III: The Discovery

The next day was Sunday, and in spite of the heavily shuttered windows, cracks of sunlight and the energetic chirping of birds contributed to keeping John from sleeping past eight o'clock. Breakfast in the main dining room was a lonely affair. Only an elderly gentleman and his wife shared the huge ballroom style dining room. The French doors, open around two sides of the room, allowed a cool breeze, heady with the scent of nectar-filled blossoms, to permeate the room.

John selected the continental breakfast which consisted of two baskets, one containing two hard rolls and a sweet roll and the other an apple, an orange, and one of the small, sweet bananas Tenerife is so famous for. Available for use on the rolls, were pats of mantequilla (butter) from Belgium and guava and orange marmalade from England. In spite of its simplicity, John enjoyed the breakfast immensely. The coffee was strong, and the orange juice, although not fresh, was refreshing. The rolls were good enough, so that the thought of opening a bakery in New York, where these could be sold, crossed his mind. He knew Irene would share his fondness for them and made a mental note to request some to take back when he was ready to leave.

The other two occupants of the dining room appeared to be German. The lady was apparently a bit deaf as her husband spoke rather loudly and repeated himself frequently.

After breakfast, John inquired of the desk clerk, "Can you tell me what time the car rental shop down the street opens, por favor?"

The clerk answered, "It is already open sir, but will close at 11:30."

John thanked him and then said, "By the way, I thought I spotted a friend here last night. Could you tell me if a Mr. Wayne Morrison is registered here?"

The clerk checked the entries in his small metal file box and answered, "No Sir, we do not have any record of a Mr. Morrison."

"Thank you," replied John.

After returning briefly to his room, where he collected his camera equipment, he strode briskly out the main entrance of the hotel and down the street, where he readily located the car rental establishment. The man on duty spoke English well and a VW Beetle was negotiated. John was told he could park the car on the street that ran beside the hotel each evening. If no parking space was available there, he could park on any of the side streets that did not specifically have a "No Aparcar" sign. He was also given a map of the island of Tenerife with a more detailed map of Santa Cruz on the reverse side.

Santa Cruz was enticing from the standpoint of history and scenic photographic opportunities. It faced the ocean and was backed by picturesque hills. Still, he remembered the mountain road leading to the villages of La Laguna and Tacoronte and the caves that could be found at the higher elevations.

These caves were purported to have been inhabited by the earliest occupants of the islands, the Guanches. He was anxious to explore and photograph them.

He located the Autopista and headed northwest toward La Laguna. In Tenerife it is customary, if you are driving fast on a divided four lane highway, to keep to the left lane and to keep your headlights on. John was in no hurry, but he couldn't resist joining the line of cars with their headlights on. After fifteen minutes of fast driving, he began to see the housing estates for workers on the right, a cemetery on his left, and an orphanage on a hill to the right. At this point he slowed for the entrance to La Laguna where the Autopista, the Old Road, and the road to La Esperanza met. Here there was an open space containing the statue of a priest, Padre Jose de Anchieta, a famous missionary from a Basque family who was born in La Laguna in 1534. He, it is said, helped found the cities of Sao Paulo and Rio de Janeiro in Brazil.

Villages and towns in Tenerife and the other Canary Islands, and indeed in most of the Spanish mainland as well, are proud of their heritage. La Laguna was no exception. It was the first capital of the archipelago, having been founded on the banks of a small lagoon. There was no longer a lagoon, however, as it was drained about the middle of the eighteenth century.

John thought about stopping to photograph some of the striking Spanish colonial style buildings with their magnificent doors and emblazoned façades. Still, he was intent on taking advantage of the clear atmosphere and felt this would be an exceptional day to photograph the scenery at higher altitudes.

He drove on past the University of La Laguna and into town, taking the first fork along the Calle de Santo Domingo.

Shortly he arrived at an old Dominican monastery which is now a Diocesan Seminary. Here he stopped briefly to photograph a dragon tree which was acclaimed to be 2000 years old. It was most luxuriant and almost perfect in shape, a beautiful specimen of an almost extinct species.

Leaving La Laguna, John followed a road lined with magnificent eucalyptus trees, up to a higher elevation. When he reached the villages of Las Canteras and Las Mercedes, he found the roadside planted with Canary Cedars. He stopped to take pictures of the surrounding countryside. La Laguna could be seen below on one side and Santa Cruz in the distance on the other side. The weather was clear, and he had a wonderful view of the peak of Mount Teide. This is the island's famous volcano which has been dormant since its last eruption in 1909.

Continuing through the Mercedes Forest, John's little VW climbed up along part of the Anaga Range of mountains to the mirador, or look-out point, of the Pico del Ingles, 3182 feet above sea level. After taking several pictures of the breathtaking view, John returned down the same road. Upon again reaching the village of Las Canteras, he turned off to the right on a road which led down into the valley of Tegueste. He knew this was where he might find old Guanche habitats as this was Guanche territory. He noticed that many of the villagers possessed the typical Guanche characteristics of blue or grey-green eyes and blonde hair. Continuing through the village of Tegueste, the road again began to climb toward Tacoronte which was the capital of an ancient Guanche King.

As John drove around a bend in the narrow road, he spotted a network of stone viaducts crossing the valley below. He knew these to be of Roman origin and wanted to photograph them. He was interested in them, not only from a historic standpoint, but also from an engineering viewpoint as well. He pulled his car off the road onto a bare patch of ground in a densely forested area. His car was quite out of the way of any descending or ascending vehicles. The forest floor was shaded and cool. As John's eyes became accustomed to the darkness he noticed a cave-like entrance into the solid rock face behind the trees.

In an exploratory mood, he couldn't resist investigating. He entered the cave but found that when he was but a few feet into the entrance, it was too dark to see. He returned to the car to get his flash unit and a package of matches he had noticed in the glove compartment.

As he reentered the cave, he made use of a temporary flash to show him the general direction of the deep entrance. He picked up several loose stones and tossed them ahead to assure himself that he wasn't intruding upon some wary animal who considered the cave his property. All was quiet, and he felt his way along one wall and around a bend. Another flash gave him a momentary glimpse of a sight which startled him.

There appeared to be a heavy-set man asleep on the ground.

Fishing in his pocket, he procured a match, which he lit. When he drew closer and examined the man more carefully, it was evident that the man was not asleep but dead. His first inclination was to leave immediately and forget what he had seen, but his natural curiosity and sense of duty led him to examine the body more closely. From his clothing, it appeared the man was not a local villager. He was more formally dressed. He could be a businessman. His tie was twisted unnaturally over his right shoulder, and his face was down, pushed into the floor. John turned the head gently to one side. John straightened up quickly and began to perspire profusely. Then he felt a sense of chilliness permeate his body. The man was, without a doubt, Wayne Morrison. John left the cave quickly, got into the car and drove up to Tacoronte.

At first, he entertained thoughts of forgetting what he had discovered, but these thoughts quickly vanished, and he sought out the local constabulary. He stopped in a small grocery store and asked where he could find the policio. When finally understood, he was directed to a small stone building. There he found an elderly man talking to a young policeman. He got the attention of the policeman but found his own Spanish inadequate to explain the situation. Finally, the older man asked John if he spoke English, and John was able to describe the problem to him. The man translated for the policeman, and the officer asked John to lead him to the scene of the accident. He directed John to drive his car and indicated that he would follow him.

The older man volunteered to accompany John and serve as translator. He introduced himself as he climbed into the car with John, "I'm Archy Eaton, retired British Government worker. I've been living in Tacoronte for over a year now since my retirement. You must be a tourist."

"Not entirely," replied John, starting the engine and driving slowly back down the road toward the cave. "I'm an engineer from New York working for Amco. I'm in Santa Cruz researching some production problems for our factory here. My hobby is photography which explains why I look like a tourist. I've been indulging myself today by recording some of your breathtaking scenery."

"Sounds as if you've found yourself some scenery you'd rather not have discovered," Archy averred wryly.

"Yes, and even worse, I know the man, in a way. He sat next to me on the plane from New York to Madrid.

"That is a coincidence. Where did the man come from?"

"From New York."

"Was he an American too?"

"Yes, he told me he intended to purchase goods for the business he owned in New York. I can't imagine how he came to be here in Tenerife. He specifically mentioned that he was traveling only to Madrid, Toledo, and Seville on this trip."

Archy asked John if he knew the cause of the man's death.

"I have no idea how he died," answered John. "I didn't want to disturb the body further without first informing the police."

"Perhaps," interjected Archy, "he changed his mind and decided to take a break from his job and become a tourist for the weekend. He probably died from some natural cause such as a sudden heart attack."

"That may be so," speculated John doubtfully, "But he seemed a bit young for a heart attack. It's not impossible of course."

"Perhaps he met with some sort of accident," countered Archy.

"If he had an accident, how did he get into the cave? I shouldn't think if anyone else were involved in his accidental death that they would have carried him into the cave, and he certainly wouldn't have dragged himself in there if he were injured. I wonder if he could have met with foul play?"

"That's possible; we shall see!" replied Archy.

John, reaching the small, forested area in front of the cave, signaled for a turn and pulled the car to a halt, leaving room for the policeman's vehicle in the small clearing. He and Archy alighted and stood waiting for the policeman and the two villagers who accompanied him, to remove themselves from their car.

"Did you discover the man in here?" queried the policeman in a somewhat skeptical tone.

"Yes, let me show you. You'll need a flashlight. The cave is very dark."

The policeman returned to his car for a moment to select a good-sized electric lantern. He switched this on as he entered the cave. From the tone of his exclamation when he located the body, John felt sure that the disbelieving policeman was now a believer.

The policeman turned the body over completely and examined it roughly and somewhat superficially. He probed the pockets of Wayne's jacket and trousers and unbuttoned his shirt and belt. As he removed the jacket, all the men could see the cause of death. A bullet hole had penetrated the right side of the victim's chest from the front and traversed completely through to the back. Wayne's shirt back was a mass of clotted, dried blood, as was the inside back lining of his jacket.

"It looks as if your hunch was right," said Archy as he helped the policeman move the body again.

Because there was no hole in the jacket, John speculated that Wayne had been shot when he was not wearing the coat, and that the coat had been put on after his death. This was verified by the fact that Wayne's shirt sleeves were rolled up to above his elbows. It was unlikely that a man would put a suit jacket on over rolled-up sleeves, himself. He would be more likely to roll the sleeves down and button them first.

John kept these speculations to himself.

If the policeman noticed these facts, he did not mention them. He found no form of identification in any of Wayne's pockets. Even the labels had been torn from his coat, shirt, underwear, and tie. His shoes were missing. There was no question but that a crime had been committed.

Whoever had committed the crime had counted on a delay in identification, even if the body was discovered.

Translating the policeman's conclusion, Archy informed John that this man had undoubtedly been murdered, and that the body must be taken to the city morgue for further investigation.

John offered to photograph the body in place before its removal. This offer was accepted with a smile and a bow by the officer. John took several face-up pictures of Wayne and then the policeman and his two helpers turned the body back to its original position and replaced the coat. John took several more flash photos, with the corpse in that position.

"The morgue," Archy informed John, "will be in the wine cellar under my house. I live in the largest villa in Tacoronte and the only one with a wine cellar. It has been used once before for this purpose. The deceased was an accident victim and they had to hold him until his family could be located. There is, of course, a wine cellar behind the restaurant," he added, with a twinkle in his eyes, "but I doubt that it would be good for restaurant business to use that for the morgue."

John had the feeling that the rest of the party did not view this crime in as shocking and horrible a light as he did. He felt, rather, that they looked upon it as an exciting event, perhaps even a welcome respite from the usual uneventful daily life of the village.

A blanket was removed from the trunk of the police car and the body was lifted, with the help of all five of the men, onto the blanket and carried to the car. The body was obviously not going to fit very well in the car. The only way to carry it in the car would be to hold it in an upright sitting position in the back seat and no one seemed to want to be the one to occupy the seat next to the corpse.

A solution was finally arrived at when they tied the blanket around the body with two trouser belts, one of which belonged to the victim, and strapped it over the hood of the car tied to the headlights with two other belts belonging to the villagers.

If the situation had not been so serious, John would have found it as amusing as a Peter Sellers' movie. John, who was an avid reader of mystery stories, just couldn't believe this was happening.

With everyone resettled in the two cars, the policeman's car leading the way this time, they all drove slowly back up to the village. The policeman honked intermittent blasts of his horn all the way.

When they reached the village, the noise drew a crowd, including numerous children and barking dogs. Everyone crowded around, and there was excited jabbering in Spanish concerning the blanketed bundle over the hood. When some of the questions were answered by the policeman, the voices grew quiet and widened eyes became more serious. With authoritative gestures, the policeman ordered the bystanders out of the way, and the car proceeded slowly to the police station.

At the station, the policeman made several phone calls and then returned to the cars and ordered John to follow the police car further. Archy explained to John, "As I predicted, my wine cellar must serve as a morgue. The policeman has informed the Inspector General of the district of the tragedy. He is sending some of his men and the police doctor from Santa Cruz to help with the investigation."

When they arrived at Archy's house his wife was waiting, having received advanced notice of their arrival from the telephone operator. She invited John and Archy to come into the kitchen for coffee. The policeman was also invited and agreed to come as soon as the corpse was properly stored.

Willing hands from the village helped unstrap the body and carry it carefully down into the wine cellar and place it on the table in the middle of the cellar. This necessitated removing a few empty wine bottles.

The policeman entered Archy's house, and after accepting a cup of coffee, sat down at the table and opened a large black notebook, which he had brought from the car. With Archy serving as translator, he asked John his full name, the name of his company, his home address, and his address in Tenerife. He asked, also, why John had been in the cave, where he had discovered the body, and if he had ever seen the victim before.

John explained how he had met Wayne. The policeman wrote all the information carefully in his notebook. He made several comments on the coincidental aspects of John's discovery. After John had given him the names of Antonio and Guillermo, he called Srs. Sedena and Ceballos at their homes in Santa Cruz. After what seemed like a very long conversation, the policeman handed the phone to John.

Antonio was on the other end of the line and most sympathetic, "What has happened to you is terrible. Don't be worried. I have assured the policeman that your reputation is impeccable, and I will call my lawyer as soon as I am off the phone. I will also phone the chief judge in Santa Cruz. He is my father's cousin. You won't have to worry about a thing. The policeman says you are free to return to Santa Cruz as soon as the Inspector General arrives and signs a release for you. Do you want me to come and get you?"

"No thank you," assured John, "I have a rented car and can drive back to Santa Cruz myself. I would like to take another look at the cave on the way back. I shall call you when I arrive back at the hotel."

"It is a good idea not to get too involved. The men from the Inspector General's office will carry out a very thorough investigation."

"If the evidence is not completely obliterated by the many sightseers and would-be helpers," John thought to himself. Out loud John agreed with Antonio that perhaps it would be better if he left the investigating entirely to the authorities.

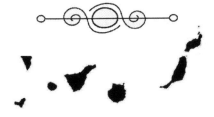

Marilyn Joyce Lafferty Sietsema

CHAPTER IV: The Trip Back

It was after six o'clock in the evening before Inspector General de Lugo arrived. He was an older man with thinning gray hair. His countenance was formal and a bit stern. His slender, straight body indicated his military training. Sharp, piercing eyes twinkled above thin lips, topped by a well-trimmed mustache. He spoke English with a definite British accent, suggesting he had spent some time in Great Britain. English is taught in almost all schools in the Canary Islands but usually by people with a strong Spanish accent.

"I understand you have encountered some trouble," he stated briefly, in keeping with his taciturn manner.

"Yes," replied John. "I came upon a cave while taking pictures at a look-out point. I decided to explore the cave and discovered the body of a man in it. This was the same man who sat next to me on the plane from New York yesterday. I would not have expected him to be in the Canary Islands, as he had specifically mentioned that he would only be in Madrid, and possibly Seville or Toledo during this trip."

John felt that it was definitely an advantage to be able to speak to the Inspector General directly instead of through Archy as a translator. Archy seemed to be a good-natured fellow and probably was an accurate translator, but it was always disconcerting to give a detailed explanation and have it reiterated in Spanish with just a few words. Or in some instances, John would give a short single sentence explanation only to have it take a good two or three minutes to translate into Spanish. John did not feel he was in control of his communication in these instances.

The Inspector General made no comment but asked him to repeat his story of the discovery of Wayne Morrison's body while a secretary typed his statement rapidly on her portable typewriter. After giving and signing the statement, John was told that he was free to drive back to Santa Cruz. He said goodbye to Archy Eaton and thanked him for his help and support.

"Wouldn't you like to have dinner with me before driving back to Santa Cruz?" asked Archy. "We have an excellent little restaurant that serves superb paella and has a marvelous wine cellar."

"No thank you. I want to rest up a bit before starting work tomorrow. Perhaps we can have dinner another time."

"I can understand your being tired. The tension involved in your gruesome discovery would be likely to mentally exhaust anyone. You have remained remarkably calm. Yes, let's get together another time. I'll walk you to your car."

Climbing into his car for the return drive, John thought about his friend Wayne and wondered what clues he might find if he returned to the cave on his way back to Santa Cruz. He suspected that this was not a good idea, but he decided to return to the cave anyway. He needed a source of light so stopped at the local grocery and supply store in Tacoronte to purchase a flashlight. As he searched among the available goods for sale, he felt stares of curiosity from the storekeeper and other customers. He didn't feel that these looks were necessarily warm and friendly, and regretted not going on to Tequeste to find the flashlight he needed. The thought crossed his mind that one of the residents of Tacoronte could have been responsible for Wayne's death. If this were so, it might make the guilty one nervous to see John purchasing a flashlight. It would be of no use to suggest that he was purchasing the flashlight in case he had trouble with his car on the way back to Santa Cruz. He couldn't speak Spanish well enough to get this idea across, and as far as he could tell, no one in the store spoke English. He gave the correct number of pesetas to the shopkeeper, accepted the flashlight and four batteries and left the store.

As he climbed into the car, he resolved to keep a sharp lookout for anyone following him. After he thought about this for a while, he realized that no one would need to follow him. Anyone, with any intelligence and a knowledge of what actually happened to Wayne, would suspect that he might be returning to the cave. They could visually follow the headlights of his car by watching the road down from Tacoronte. He thought that they might even be able to determine if his car stopped at the cave site.

With these thoughts foremost in his mind, he drove carefully down the mountain road. The road was difficult enough during the day when sharp curves could be detected before they were reached. At night, these curves became a real menace. Most roads in the islands were narrow by American standards, although they were adequate for the small cars usually driven on Tenerife.

It was the custom, when approaching a sharp curve, to honk one's horn to warn drivers coming from the opposite direction. The car on the inside lane was expected to pull off the road to permit the car on the outside to pass. That this procedure was not always followed was verified by the small shrines, placed at intervals, along the road. Some shrines contained photos of the luckless drivers who had been killed at that particular spot in the road. Frequently, a vase of flowers was seen on a shrine, placed there by the loved ones of the unfortunate traffic victim. These shrines were meant, not only as memorials, but as warnings to current drivers to limit their speed on the curves.

John carefully honked at each blind curve and could hear the echoes of his honks reverberating from the surrounding hills. Still concerned that his progress down the mountain could readily be monitored, he made the decision to continue past the spot where he had discovered the cave. He continued to honk at curves until he reached the valley. There he turned off his headlights, turned his car around, and slowly drove back up the mountain to the cave site. On this return trip he did not honk his horn. Pulling his car off the road at the small clearing in front of the cave, he turned off the engine, rolled down the window on the driver's side, and listened carefully for almost fifteen minutes. He heard nothing suspicious. No car passed on the road, and there were no sounds but the occasional scurry of some small animal, the distant lowing of domestic animals, or the sounds of the villages in the valley below.

When he finally dislodged himself from the car, he felt stiff and sore and realized how tense he had been while waiting and listening. He closed the door of the car softly and felt his way to the cave. A partial moon, which shone brightly overhead, aided his progress. Only when he was inside did he risk using the flashlight. He located the spot where Wayne's body had been. There was still a small brown spot where blood had soaked into the dirt. The fact that there wasn't a great deal of blood further substantiated his speculation that the murder had not occurred in the cave.

He examined footprints on the dirt floor of the cave but could not be sure that they had not all been made by the police and other observers. He was able to find one of his own prints intact. He knew it was his because he compared it with his own current prints. He could find no indications that the body had been dragged into the cave, nor was there evidence that anyone had brushed or swept away such marks. This meant that someone had carried Wayne in. Because of Wayne's size, he reasoned that one person, even a very strong one, would have had difficulty carrying him. Most likely, two or more carriers were involved.

Actually, although there were many footprints, some on top of each other, and some indistinct, there were enough clear prints in the loose dust that John decided to photograph as many clear prints as possible. Altogether, he took pictures of 17 distinct, different prints. He reasoned that these might, or might not, be useful at some later date. He felt it was better to have some information that might not prove useful than to miss an important clue. John was a detail man and a curious one. He had made up his mind to try and determine what had happened to Wayne.

Although he ventured further into the cave and examined the floor and the walls carefully, he found no other useful evidence. He spent almost an hour in the cave and then decided he had better not delay returning to the hotel. An interested person could easily check the time of his return there.

After leaving the cave, he did risk being seen by using his flashlight to look for tire tracks. There were only his own tracks and those of the police car. However, upon examination of the opposite side of the road, where he had taken pictures of the landscape in the morning, he discovered two additional sets of tracks. He used his flash to photograph these, wishing he had infrared film and flash. He realized that these tire tracks could be from the cars of other tourists, but the pictures would be available later if needed.

He began to feel uncomfortable; probably paranoia setting in, he guessed. He hurriedly climbed back into the car, started the engine, and drove quickly back down to the valley below. As he reached a spot, just before the village of Tequeste, where the road in front of the cave could be seen, he slowed and glanced back. What he saw sent a slight shiver through his body. He saw car headlights for a brief second, and then they were gone. They could have vanished because the driver turned the next bend, or more than likely, he thought, they had been turned on briefly and then off.

Needless to say, John did not stop in Tequeste, but drove rapidly on up the mountain on the other side to Las Canteras and then descended again to La Laguna. Here he picked up the Autopista and drove back to Santa Cruz. He felt safer on this main highway with its continuing stream of banana trucks on their way to deliver perishable products to the docks of Santa Cruz.

He stopped in Santa Cruz for gasoline and then returned to the Mencey. He enquired again if Wayne Morrison had registered at the hotel. A different clerk checked, and the results were the same; no one by that name had been registered within the past week.

It was at this point that John realized that no one had asked for the film he had with the pictures he had taken of Wayne's body in the cave. He realized that perhaps the register clerk would recognize Wayne under another name if he could see his picture. He also realized that if anyone was concerned enough, they might make some attempt to get the film from him.

He therefore went to his room, removed the latest roll of film from his camera, placed this roll, along with the one he had exposed earlier for the police, in the film mailers he had brought with him from the States. He put his wife's return address on them, so they would be returned to New York after they were processed.

He went downstairs to the hotel desk and discovered that the mail would not be taken to the post office until noon of the next day. Impulsively, he left the security of the hotel, drove to the post office in the center of town and dropped the film mailers into the night mailbox. The task took only 15 minutes, and he encountered no problems. Returning to his room, he felt much more confident and safe.

Only after he reached his room did he realize how hungry he was. He had not eaten since breakfast. Since dining does not usually begin until 10:00 in Santa Cruz, he had plenty of time to wash, dress and enjoy a full and satisfying meal in the main dining room. He indulged himself with his favorite items al la carte. He ordered creamed spinach, which could have been a meal in itself. It arrived in a large family sized bowl and was delectable. It must have contained at least two bunches of cooked spinach, with butter, cream, and flour to bind it together, and just a hint of onion, nutmeg, and pepper to enhance the fresh spinach flavor. He ate this with the crusty hard rolls for which all of Spain is famous. He then ordered roast lamb and finally ended the meal with a smooth, light flan, and a cup of strong black coffee. This last item he didn't finish as he wanted to get a good night's sleep.

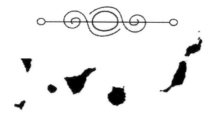

CHAPTER V: A Surprise Meeting

When John awoke the next morning, it seemed as if Sunday's adventure must have been a fleeting nightmare. He knew this was not so, but in the rush to get dressed and have breakfast, before heading for Amco, he had little time to think about it.

As he entered the Amco Plant, Antonio's secretary, Rosa, greeted him and said that Antonio would like to see him. When John entered the office, Antonio was at his desk. He welcomed John and asked how he was feeling after his ordeal. He mentioned that he had just had a call from Inspector General Fernandez de Lugo. "He is sending one of his aides to pick up the film which has the photographs you took of Mr. Morrison in the cave. He says that you must also sign the statement that you dictated last night," explained Antonio.

"But I already signed the statement last night."

"Ah, but this is a copy which has been edited with respect to typing and spelling errors and retyped."

John shook his head and laughed. "The Inspector General sounds like a perfectionist to me."

"He is. He also has had a picture of the dead man taken and printed. He wants you to sign this for identification purposes. The aide will probably not be here until this afternoon. De Lugo has assured me that you are in no way suspect, and that he will probably not have to bother you again. You will not likely even be needed at the inquest."

John acknowledged Antonio's information but didn't mention that he had already mailed the film off to the United States. He knew he would not be very popular with the Inspector General when this was discovered. Still, last night it had seemed like the right thing to do. He supposed he should call Inspector General de Lugo right away and explain the situation, but he was afraid that there might still be time to regain the film from the post office. How could he be sure that local interests would not prompt someone to destroy the film or remove some evidence of vital importance from the negatives or pictures?

The truth of the matter was that John did not know exactly who could be trusted. Besides, it was unlikely the police would recover only the one mailer which contained the pictures he took for the police and not come upon the other which contained those pictures he had taken on his way back to the hotel last night. In this case, he would have to explain that he was interested in the case and investigating it on his own. All in all, this was an awkward situation, and John decided to give the mailers every opportunity to leave the Island and be on their way to the States. There he knew the film would get impartial treatment and could not possibly be tampered with.

He would phone Irene this evening and arrange with her to call the photo lab and have them make duplicates, not only of the pictures, but of the negatives as well. Then they could mail the originals to Irene and the duplicates to him. This way, if the photos were, in some way, altered or destroyed, he could be sure the originals were safe.

Antonio showed John to the small office which would be his during his stay in Santa Cruz. He also introduced him to Maria Albareda, a student who would serve for the next few weeks as his interpreter. She was a very attractive young lady and seemed most intelligent. She was not dressed in the same formal manner as Rosa and Alberina but seemed to belong to a different generation, although she was about their age. Maria had long, dark, straight hair. She was quite slender and wore tight fitting jeans with a casual sweater drawn tautly across her full, well developed breasts. John asked Maria what she was studying at the University.

"I am studying the Spanish language and Spanish history," she replied, in an American dialect which suggested that her home might be in the Southern part of the United States.

When John asked her where she was from, she replied, "Well, I was raised in Dallas, Texas but have been living with my aunt in New York City for the past four years. Since September, I have been studying here in Tenerife. I, of course, live at the university dormitory in La Laguna."

"You are working while attending school?"

"No, classes will not resume after the Christmas vacation until the first of February. They are, fortunately, letting me stay at the dorm during the vacation period." Further discussion revealed that Maria's Aunt was supplying the money for her education and expected frequent reports on her progress.

The first task John had for Maria was to translate and type up in English some reports from the mainland, from Madrid, to be exact. These reports depicted how the Amco products, manufactured here in Tenerife, had been selling. While she was doing this, John went with Antonio out to the factory. Amco, short for The American Company, was introducing several products into Spain. The first products to be manufactured in Tenerife and supplied to the Spanish mainland were a line of wafer bars. Antonio and John stood for a while and watched the bars being covered with caramel and then chocolate as they were carried along on the conveyor belt. After careful observation, John could see that the temperatures were too high in both the caramel and the chocolate vats. This was evident because of the slightly burned odor emitting into the room. He checked the temperatures and confirmed what he had suspected. Consumers in Madrid and several other towns where the candies were distributed had been complaining about bad product flavor. John felt certain that the elevated temperatures were the cause.

John was up and down ladders, checking machinery and gauges and asking questions of the operators of the machinery. Antonio translated for him. Later, when Antonio had to leave, Maria was called from the office and served as translator. She seemed very astute about understanding his questions and interpreting the answers of the workers. He even, at times, preferred her to Antonio as she didn't edit the worker's replies as he expected Antonio may have done. Antonio would not necessarily do this consciously, but it was second nature to him to want John to believe that all aspects of the plant were running well, in spite of the fact that he and his brother had called John in because they were having problems.

It wasn't until three in the afternoon that Inspector General de Lugo's aide arrived. The statement had been typed in both Spanish and English. John read the English copy and then had Maria read the Spanish version, translating it into English as she read it out loud. Both versions seemed to approximate his perception of the incident, so he signed and returned them to the aide. He did notice that no mention was made of Wayne's name. He was, throughout the report, referred to as "the deceased". Perhaps this was an oversight on the part of the police, or perhaps they were investigating the possibility of another name for Wayne.

Maria commented while he was signing the statement, "Mr. Dunn, this must have been a frightening experience for you."

"It was certainly more than I was prepared for when I went out to enjoy a day of photographing the scenery," John replied.

At this time, the aide pulled out an 8 x 10 inch glossy, black and white photograph of Wayne. It had obviously been taken with flash in Archy Eaton's wine cellar. Two wine bottles could be seen beside the table which was being used as a mortuary slab. He handed the picture to John with instructions to Maria to have him sign the statement on the back which indicated that this was a picture of the body of the man found in the cave the day before.

Maria explained and then looked over John's shoulder as he put the photo on his desk, picture side up. As he was about to turn the picture over, John heard a slight gasp and looked up at Maria to find her pale and looking very ill and frightened.

She turned away quickly and pretended to arrange some papers and books on the bookcase shelf behind the desk. The aide apparently did not notice her gasp or paleness, so John decided not to comment. He placed his signature in the proper place, rose from his chair, and returned the photo to the aide, at the same time leading him toward the door of the office.

As he reached the door, the aide turned and asked for the roll of film. Maria quickly recovered from her state of shock and translated the request. John explained that he had sent the roll to the States for proper processing and that he would personally take it to Inspector General de Lugo as soon as he received it. He explained that he had used a special kind of film and that he had been afraid that no one in Tenerife would have the special chemicals to process it adequately. He sincerely hoped that the Inspector General and those on his staff knew very little about photography. The aide accepted the answer, bowed slightly, turned, and left the office.

After John had casually closed the door he turned to Maria, who was quietly crying, and asked, "Why are you so upset Maria? Did you recognize the man in the photo?"

"I guess I have just never seen a picture of a dead man before," she sobbed, almost silently.

"Maria, don't try to fool me. You are more upset than someone who has seen a picture of a body for the first time. Do you know this man? What is his name?'"

As her sobs became less easily suppressed, John patted her shoulder in a fatherly manner and finally elicited her reply. "He was my lover! I have known him since the first week in

September when we met on the Iberian plane that brought us both from Madrid."

This information surprised John as he recalled Wayne's statement that he was seriously interested in a young lady from New York. Of course, Maria did say she had been living in New York for the past four years. Perhaps the woman Wayne had referred to was Maria. Still, he had not mentioned that she was a student attending school in Tenerife. Either Wayne had two women he was interested in, or he had some reason for not wanting anyone to know he had an interest in the Canary Islands.

In retrospect, Wayne's disappearance at the airport in Madrid was singular, as was his unexplained brief appearance at the hotel. John concluded that he probably had some reason for not wanting anyone to know of his activities on Tenerife. It was very likely that his activities in Tenerife were, in some way, connected with his demise.

For the present, he would assume that Maria and the girl Wayne had discussed with him on the plane were one and the same person. He decided he would not disclose Wayne's mentioning his fondness for a certain young lady to Maria, at least not for the moment.

John asked Maria to tell him exactly when she had met Wayne and as much about their relationship as she could. At first, she seemed reluctant, but when John told her he was investigating Wayne's death on his own and would be obliged to turn the information of her relationship over to the Inspector General if she did not cooperate, her attitude changed. She agreed to start from the beginning and tell him everything.

"I first met Wayne last September on an Iberian plane coming from Madrid. I was on my way here to attend school. It was that one o'clock flight that arrives in Tenerife about three hours after leaving Madrid. We were seated next to each other. He seemed to be a friendly man and he asked me if I was on a vacation trip to the Canary Islands. I explained that I was going to be a student at the University of La Laguna. He seemed interested in my studies and was impressed by the fact that I would be taking courses in language and history," she said.

After a sob or two, she continued, "He was very kind and friendly and when we landed, suggested that we share a cab. He insisted that the taxi driver take us first to La Laguna. Not only did he accompany me to the University, he waited while I registered at the dormitory. The lady who assigned my room seemed to think he was a relative." She smiled faintly, "Neither of us said anything to correct her conclusion."

"What happened then?" questioned John.

"He finally left me in La Laguna, after making sure I was well taken care of. He said he would call me as soon as he was settled at the Hotel Mencey where he was planning to stay," she replied.

"Did he give you any idea what he was doing in Tenerife?" John asked.

"Yes, on the plane and during the drive to La Laguna he mentioned that he was in the importing business. His primary job was to search for unique items from exotic places that could be sold through sophisticated catalogs and in fine specialty shops. One time, when we were on a date, he told me that most of the things he bought would sell for a great deal of money in the stores," she answered.

"You saw him frequently after that then?" suggested John.

"Oh yes," she continued, "For the next two weeks he called me at least once a day. Whenever I could afford the time, we had lunch or dinner together, went to movies, and even attended several bullfights. I didn't like these very much, but I didn't want to hurt Wayne's feelings, as he had gone to some trouble to get tickets and seemed to enjoy going himself."

As she further remembered, "He would frequently be away from Tenerife, back in the States, and in other countries for six to eight weeks. During these times I missed him. We would write each other, of course, but I always felt depressed when he was away. We gradually fell very much in love."

"How intimate did your relationship become?" queried John.

"We spent weekends together whenever we could arrange it. Mostly, we would stay at hotels in Puerto de La Cruz. Once we even drove up to the lodge near the top of Mount Teide," Marie acknowledged almost shyly.

"How did you explain your weekend absences to the dormitory matron?" inquired John.

"My girlfriends at the University let me use their homes as my supposed weekend destinations. They planned to say I was with them if anyone asked, but no one ever checked on me," she responded.

"How did your aunt feel about your relationship with Wayne?"

"I never told her about our relationship. She is kind of old fashioned and would have been furious. If she had even known that I was dating a boy, she would, most likely, have been angry and would certainly have insisted I return to New York. Wayne and I were in love. We planned to become engaged in the future. We weren't sure, even then, that we would tell my aunt immediately. As it was, she thought I was a proper young lady with no real temptations in Tenerife. Wayne and I planned to be married eventually and then tell her," Maria sobbed, before adding, "We were going to have our wedding in the Cathedral at Candelaria."

"You say you live with your aunt when you are in New York? What about your parents?"

"My mother and father still live in Dallas, but they are divorced. Neither of them has much interest in me. My mother is a fashion designer. I used to see her on occasion when she came to New York, but she felt I was better off living in New York with my aunt who doesn't have a career. My father is a broker and, as such, is very busy. In addition, he has a variety of girlfriends and I'm sure I would have cramped his lifestyle if I had decided to reside with him. Auntie isn't really a bad person. She never married and consequently has no children of her own. I guess I'm pretty lucky. She treats me as if I were her own daughter. It's just that she is not young anymore and doesn't understand the younger generation."

"Is there anything else you can tell me? Did Wayne ever mention anything about his family?"

"No, not really, "replied Maria. "I know his mother lives in Fort Wayne, Indiana. She is a widow as his father died of a heart attack when Wayne was 19. Wayne was 33 years old, had never been married and lived in an apartment on Manhattan."

"Do you have his address?" returned John.

"Not his apartment address, but I do have his business address." she replied, "I sent the letters I wrote there. That way Wayne could be certain they would be forwarded to him wherever he was working." She wrote the address on a slip of paper and handed it to John.

John looked at the slip of paper briefly and tucked it in his pocket. He noted that it was a P.O. box address. "Did he ever give you his home address, or do you know his mother's address?" continued John.

"No," replied Maria.

"I suppose the police will be able to find both. When they discover his mother's address, I'm sure they will inform her of her son's death," muttered John, half under his breath. "What about Wayne's company? Did he ever mention the name or in what part of New York it was located?"

Maria confirmed what John already knew. "The name of his company was the World-Wide Import Export Company. The P.O. Box address is the only company address I have. I am not really familiar with that part of town, so I can't say, even in a general way, where his office is located. I don't think he ever mentioned his mother's address. He would have had no reason to give it to me, as I had not thought about writing her. In many ways, he seemed such a private person. He never wanted to talk about himself very much, and I didn't feel I had a right to pry, although I was curious about his background and family," said Maria, somewhat wistfully.

"All right," sighed John. "We have work to do. I'm going to arrange for you to stay with Antonio's wife for the remainder of your vacation. It may not be safe for you to remain in the dormitory, especially when there are few people around. I don't know why Wayne was killed or who shot him, and I have no way of telling whether or not your having known him will put you in danger. It is possible that whoever killed Wayne may think it necessary to kill you too, especially if they are aware that you and I know each other. One last question; did Wayne ever mention the names of any of his contacts here? Did he ever introduce you to any of them?"

"No," Maria replied, somewhat sullenly, "I just loved him, I didn't nag him. I felt that he would let me know more about himself as he trusted me more."

When Maria was able to pull herself together, wash and remake her face, she went back to translating the Madrid report. "This could be a lucky break in the case, finding someone who knew Wayne," thought John. He did feel, however, that she knew more about Wayne than what she had admitted. Perhaps when she knew John better, she would be willing to tell him more.

Before retiring that evening, John called Irene. He told her about his adventure in detail. He knew she would worry, but it was necessary to keep her informed accurately if she were to understand the reason for what she must do with the film he had mailed to the photo laboratory in New York.

Besides, he wanted her to know everything, in the event that anything should happen to him. Before their phone conversation was completed, Irene and John had agreed that he would call her at least every other evening. If, for any reason, she should not hear from him, she was to call the Inspector General personally and tell him what she knew.

Irene promised to see to the film the same day. She knew the address of the laboratory where John had his film processed and would call as soon as they were through with their conversation, alert them to the film he had sent, and have them call her as soon as they received it. She told John how much she loved him and missed him and urged him to be careful. After completing the phone call, John was able to relax and slept well.

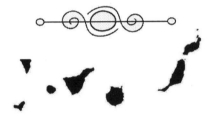

Marilyn Joyce Lafferty Sietsema

CHAPTER VI: Double Identity

The remainder of the week was busy for John. Work at the plant began early and generally lasted until around ten in the evening when everyone, including the secretaries, went out to eat and celebrate the end of a long, hard day. Sometimes Antonio's and Guillermo's wives joined them at the restaurant.

The only time John had to think about the circumstances connected with Wayne's death was during the two-hour siesta in the afternoon. During this time, he usually returned to the hotel, showered, and allowed his mind to review the case and plan his future strategy.

On Wednesday, during his afternoon break, John made further enquiries at the Mencey desk about Wayne. This time he was lucky in encountering a friendly and talkative desk clerk. This clerk also assured John that there was no one by the name of Wayne Morrison listed in the hotel register file. John asked, "Do you have any guests that you have not seen since Sunday or who have mail which has not been collected since then?"

The clerk looked dubious, but as he glanced at the file box, where his finger was still holding the place where Wayne Morrison's card would have been if he had been registered, he pulled out a card with a red clip on it. "Here is the card of a Mr. William Morton who was to be here only through Sunday. His

belongings are still in his room, and he has not checked out,"
responded the clerk.

With that, he hailed a bellboy and asked him to check on
Mr. Morton. The bellboy returned shortly and reported that the
suitcase and clothing of Mr. Morton were still in the room. He
also mentioned that he had talked to the maid, and that Mr.
Morton had not slept in or used his room since Saturday night.

John was struck by the similarity of the names. William
Morton and Wayne Morrison were very alike. He was aware that
when people used aliases, they were usually unwilling to
completely give up their own identity and frequently assumed
names with the same initials as their real names. This was
especially true of men. He discussed this with the clerk and
explained that he would like a glance at the luggage and
wardrobe of Mr. Morton to see if he was, indeed, the same man
as Mr. Morrison. The clerk was reluctant, but when John pressed
a sum of money into his hand with the suggestion that they could
both take a quick look at the contents of the room while the
bellboy kept a good watch on the elevator, the clerk acquiesced.

The three men ascended to the fifth floor in the elevator.
While the bellboy remained outside, the clerk opened the door
and he and John went inside. John looked first inside the closet
where he confirmed, indeed, that Mr. Morton owned a suit and
tie exactly like those which Wayne had worn on the plane. The
carry-on bag on the luggage rack was also exactly like the one
Wayne had carried from the plane in Madrid. There was a
matching two-suiter in the closet. John knew it would be useless
to request that the clerk open the carry-on bag to look for
identification, so he did not bother to ask. He did, however, ask

what would happen to Mr. Morton's belongings if he did not return, and they were not claimed.

The clerk replied, "They will be stored in a room downstairs where we keep the baggage of those who have neglected to pay their bills, and where we keep items that visitors have forgotten."

"How long will it be before Mr. Morton's belongings are removed from his room?" asked John.

"According to his card, Mr. Morton booked this room only through last Sunday evening. Someone else may have reserved the room beginning Monday. We probably were able to find another room for that person, but I expect the manager will remove Mr. Morton's possessions today at check-out time if we have not heard from him," asserted the clerk. He went on, with a frown, "We will then probably notify the police, sir."

"Will the police pick up his belongings?" questioned John.

"Only if a man has been reported missing. Otherwise, his things will remain here indefinitely, and after a year they will be sold to help pay his unpaid bill. We will, however, write a letter to his business address first to inform him that he has not paid his bill or picked up his luggage," noted the clerk.

John requested Mr. Morton's business address and learned that it was the World Wide Import-Export Company in New York. He copied the address and phone number in his little black book, thanked the clerk and tipped the bellboy generously. He was now certain that Morton and Morrison were one and the same person because the address of Mr. Morton's business was the same P.O. box address that Maria had used to write letters to Wayne. He hurriedly returned to the plant, planning to call his wife later to have her do some sleuthing for him stateside.

It was nearly midnight when he returned to the Mencey and put in a call to Irene. She was glad to hear his voice and happy that he was still safe. He gave her Wayne's business address and asked her to find out where he was supposed to be and where he lived. He told her about the information he had gleaned from Maria and the hotel clerk. He implored her to be careful when she enquired at Wayne's place of business. If she was asked her name, she was to give a fictitious one. Irene agreed and said she would find out what she could. He spent the remainder of their conversation reassuring her that he was in no danger and would be extra careful and only venture out with friends after dark. Fond goodbyes were said, and John fell asleep quickly after climbing into bed. This was a rare achievement considering the lumpy condition of the hotel mattress.

Thursday morning, he revealed his findings to Maria.

Tears filled her eyes at his disclosures. They both wondered why Wayne had used another name. John asked Maria if she had ever wondered whether or not Wayne had a wife and if their relationship could be philanderous on Wayne's part. She tearfully replied that she didn't think Wayne was the kind of person to engage in a love affair without serious intent. John assured Maria that he had no reason to suspect that Wayne had a wife. He just wanted to consider all the possibilities. Upon more extensive questioning, Maria did reveal a few additional facts which John felt might prove helpful in the case.

"Wayne did spend quite a bit of time in a town named Orotava," disclosed Maria. "One evening we went to a restaurant in that town and several patrons seemed to know him by name. When I mentioned to him that he seemed to know many people there, he laughed and said he had frequent business dealings in the town. He said he bought handmade lace and knitted items from a number of the women and handmade fishing nets from the men."

"One other time, I happened to see an oil painting in the trunk of Wayne's car. I admired it, and he mentioned the name of the artist. I can't seem to remember his name. Wayne did acknowledge that he regularly purchased paintings from him though. I do wish I could remember the man's name or where he is located. Perhaps if I concentrate, I will."

"Did you know that Wayne was in Tenerife last week?" asked John.

"No, I hadn't heard from him, but I'm sure I would have if he hadn't been killed," replied Maria with tears again welling up in her eyes. "You have got to find out who did this terrible thing."

John thought that Maria seemed to have more confidence in him now. She no longer seemed reluctant to confide in him and was eager to reveal anything which might help John in his investigation.

"He also spent some time in Candelaria," she continued after a few minutes, "In fact, he mentioned taking several trips to coastal villages. Many of the local cottage industries are located in the places he visited on Tenerife. One other thing; he must have been interested in boating. Several times I noticed he had boating gear stowed in his car, a slicker, life jacket, waterproof floating lantern, and he always carried a waterproof cigarette lighter."

At this point it came to John's mind that he too had observed that Wayne was wearing a very expensive, waterproof marine watch, the variety frequently used by scuba divers. He had seen enough Jacque Cousteau documentaries to recognize it. It was also an interesting point that there was no watch on Wayne's wrist when John found him in the cave.

John asked Maria what kind of car Wayne drove. She answered that it was a different car almost every time he picked her up as he rented cars when he needed them.

John suggested that Maria and he drive down to Orotava the following Sunday and do some scouting to see what they could learn. Maria seemed happy about this, and John noted that for the rest of the week she seemed more cheerful than at any time since Wayne's death.

John called Irene Thursday night to find out if she had learned anything from her investigation. She confirmed that Wayne was, indeed, connected with the World Wide Import-Export Company. He didn't, however, have a full-time secretary. World Wide made use of an answering service. This service included taking telephone messages and calling them to Wayne's home phone twice a day if he was there or mailing messages to him twice a week if he were out of the country and had left an address. The same service picked up his mail from a local post office box and forwarded it to his home or an out-of-town address whenever he requested them to do so.

Irene had also acquired Wayne's New York home address and phone number from the answering service. John didn't think that address sounded as if it would be in an especially good neighborhood but then it was difficult to tell about buildings in New York. It was not uncommon to have a luxury apartment building located right next to a rather run-down one. Irene planned to visit the address during an extra-long lunch break the following day.

John told her to be careful.

Irene had a plan. One of her friends, who lived in their apartment building, ran a cosmetic firm. Her salespersons sold cosmetics door-to-door. Irene thought she could borrow a salesperson's kit and gain access to the apartment in question without revealing her intent or endangering herself. John agreed. He was proud of his clever and resourceful wife.

John told Irene about his plan to drive down to Orotava with Maria the following Sunday. In the meantime, they agreed that Irene would continue to find out what she could in New York. She also intended to call the photo lab where John had sent the film to see if it had arrived and if she could convince them to rush the processing and printing. Irene and John planned to talk again late Friday evening.

When John called Irene Friday evening, she was excited and bursting with news. It seems she had gone to the address given her by Wayne's answering service. It was located in Manhattan on 14th street. The neighborhood was not the best, as John had suspected. It consisted of a few very old apartment buildings standing among barren, rat infested lots whose former buildings had been torn down.

The address was for a third-floor walk-up apartment. The building, according to Irene, had probably been constructed before the turn of the century. The hallway was ill lit but newly painted. After she rang the doorbell in the entry hall on the entering floor, she had waited several minutes before she heard a woman's questioning voice answer over the tubular opening above the letter boxes. Irene told her she was from the cosmetic company, and the woman invited her up.

The woman was probably in her sixties and very pleasant. She ordered a lipstick and powder, and just for good measure, Irene gave her a free sample of perfume. The woman seemed lonely and was eager to keep Irene chatting. She gave her name as Mrs. Mary Schumacher. Irene asked her if she had any children. She replied that she had only one son who traveled a good deal in his business.

When Irene had asked what kind of business her son was in, Mrs. Schumacher said he was in the import business and showed Irene a coffee set her son had given her on her last birthday. More questioning might have put the woman on her guard, so Irene left, promising to deliver the cosmetics the following week.

John and Irene could only speculate that Wayne Morrison was Mrs. Schumacher's son and that his mother's name was different because of a second marriage. This, of course, was inconsistent with the story Wayne had given Maria about his mother living in Indiana.

Apparently, the Spanish police had not as yet confirmed their identification of Wayne. This was obvious, as neither the answering service nor Mrs. Schumacher knew about his death.

Perhaps, however, the police had learned the reason for his death. He wondered if he should give them the additional information he had, in hopes that they would respond with what they had discovered.

He knew this was what he should do, but he also feared that his information might make both Maria and himself more vulnerable than they already were. In the back of his mind still lingered the idea that some, as yet unidentified person or persons in the Tacoronte area, where he had found Wayne's body, might be involved in his death. He had, after all, been pretty sure that someone had entered the cave after him Sunday night.

Or was it his paranoid imagination that he had seen car headlights switched on briefly at the cave site when he had looked back after driving down the mountain?

It was also possible that guilt for Wayne's demise might extend even beyond Tacoronte. Although it was unlikely, it was possible that even the office of the Inspector General was corrupt. It was certainly not unknown for policemen to become involved in crime.

The problem was that he knew very little about local politics. Therefore, he could not even speculate with any semblance of accuracy. No, he decided to wait for a few more clues to surface before going to the Inspector General with the results of his amateur detective efforts. Perhaps the case would be made more clear when he received the prints from the pictures he had taken.

It worried John that no one had informed Mrs. Schumacher of her son's death, but then he reasoned that since nothing could be done about it anyway, it probably wouldn't do any harm to let the poor soul have a few more days of peace before she was subjected to the inevitable pain that would result from knowing that her son was dead.

Also, what about Wayne's alleged mother in Fort Wayne? What explanation could be given for his seeming to have two mothers?

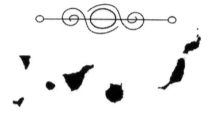

CHAPTER VII: An Unpleasant Trip

The main conveyor belt at the plant broke down Friday afternoon. The company repair crew was unable to get it started so Antonio and Guillermo declared Saturday a holiday. This was a rare occurrence in the Canary Islands, where everyone works on Saturday. Consequently, John and Maria decided to drive down to Orotava early Saturday morning instead of waiting until Sunday.

It was a bright, sparkling morning, typical weather for the Islands, when John left the hotel to pick up Maria at Antonio's house. As he headed up into the hills, the sky became overcast, and he encountered some drizzle. This was usual for the foothills in the early morning. John knew the sky would clear later and the same weather would prevail here as at the lower level in Santa Cruz.

As he drove into the driveway, he was greeted by five of Antonio's seven children. They were all studying English under the tutelage of an English student who was spending a year with Antonio and his family while studying Spanish at the Universidad de La Laguna. The children were eager to practice their English and greeted him with shouts of, "Hello!" and "Good Morning," and "My name is Estella."

Their young English tutor subdued them and apologized for their exuberance. She introduced herself as Nancy Hartford, and John noted her strong English accent and beautiful creamy complexion. She was as light complexioned, in fact, as Maria was dark. Maria appeared a few minutes later.

The girls seemed to have hit it off well. Maria explained that she was sharing a room with Nancy and liked this much better than staying in the dormitory at the University. Nancy and Maria had never met at the University, but Nancy said this was probably because she was a commuting student. "I just attend classes and then return here. I don't have much time to socialize. I am delighted to have Maria staying here."

Antonio and his wife appeared at the doorway following the girls. Nothing would do but that John should come and have breakfast with them. John protested that he had already partaken of the continental breakfast at the hotel, but Antonio waved this aside as being merely an appetizer. He insisted that John have a real breakfast with the family out on the covered patio.

They went through the house, which was large and decorated with the very latest style Spanish furniture. The living room was paved with dark brown Spanish tiles and filled with three leather sofas, six easy chairs, and an appropriate number of coffee and end tables. In one corner of the huge room was a large bar open on two sides for easy access.

Antonio asked if John would like a Bloody Mary before breakfast. John declined. He never had been able to stomach alcohol before a full day of meals. They went through the extensive, well-equipped kitchen out onto the giant patio. Here pork chops were cooking on the barbecue grill supervised by Guillermo who was wearing a tall chef's hat and an apron with a slogan indicating that he was a 'chef extraordinaire'. Some of his children were swimming in the pool and others were helping set the table.

John was not unhappy that they had persuaded him to have a second breakfast as he sat down to a delicious repast of pork chops, fresh buttered corn on the cob, croissants and sweet rolls, slices of tangy Manchego cheese, and fresh lettuce and tomato chunks, served with an olive oil and vinegar dressing.

John's plans for leaving early were further thwarted when he was invited to join a soccer game with the seven boys and four girls, plus Antonio, Guillermo, Nancy, and Maria. The game was all in fun with allowances made for everyone's mistakes.

John noted that the children played very well. They had obviously had much practice. The wives of Antonio and Guillermo watched the action from the sidelines as they were awaiting the arrival of their eighth and ninth child respectively.

It was almost noon when, with some regret, John and Maria climbed into his VW. John had asked Nancy to join them, but she refused with a knowing smile, which made John wonder what Maria had told her about their trip. Actually, he was not sorry she could not come as he was not too keen about revealing the extent of his investigations. His episode in the cave was a favorite topic of conversation but both Guillermo and Antonio assumed he was leaving all further investigating to the police.

The drive to Orotava was pleasant. They passed many banana plantations with their rows of plants in different stages of development. Several of the plantations were the background for attractive Spanish colonial houses with much carved gingerbread. John made a mental note to return and photograph these houses at a later date. He had his camera with him but hesitated to take the time to photograph them then. He wanted to get to Orotava and have time for a thorough investigation of that town and then return Maria to Antonio's at a respectable hour. They both observed and admired the riot of flowers in bloom along the roadway.

As they drove through La Victoria, on the way to Orotava, Maria remembered that she had visited a potter's house with Wayne in that town. They drove down each street of the village until Maria recognized the somewhat rundown stone house with its front yard stacked high with primitive looking ceramic bowls and pots of various shapes.

John parked the car, and they browsed among the pots and bowls as if they were tourists, until a shriveled little old lady, wearing a black dress and a black scarf over her head, appeared, to enquire in Spanish, if they had found anything they would like to buy. John priced several of the bowls and Maria advised him on which ones were most attractive. She asked for several, and the old woman helped them carry their purchases to the car.

The woman seemed friendly until Maria asked her if she had seen Wayne recently. Then the woman stopped smiling and after a few seconds of thought, recognized Maria as the girl who had been there before with Wayne. She told Maria that she had not seen him for over two months and had been wondering when he would return. Her son, it seems, had an order for several hundred custom made pots for Wayne. These were ready and waiting in the storehouse for him to pick up.

Maria translated all this for John, and by way of a head nod and a serious look, he indicated to her that she should not, at this time, disclose the fact of Wayne's death. Maria explained to the woman that she too was wondering when Wayne would return.

As they drove away, down the Roman built volcanic rock road, Wayne could see the old lady in his rear-view mirror. The moment his car pulled away she scurried into the house, a little too rapidly for such an ancient person, he thought.

The next town they drove through was Santa Ursula. Here they admired the church square with its jacarandas or rosewood trees. It was too early for the delicate blue flowers that would smother the trees from April to July.

Arriving in La Orotava, John drove directly to the restaurant where Maria and Wayne had eaten. It was too early for lunch, considering the ample and late breakfast they had had earlier. They decided, however, that this should not be a consideration.

As they entered the dimly lit, cool restaurant, they were greeted by the old gentleman who was part owner of the establishment. He recognized Maria as the young lady who had dined with Wayne and looked at John in surprise, probably wondering why it was not Wayne who was with her.

After they were seated, the old man introduced himself to John. He asked about Wayne, and Maria said she had not seen him for over a month. When she asked if the old man had talked to him recently, he replied that he had not seen him since she and he had been in together, over a month ago.

Maria asked if there were anyone else who might have seen Wayne or who might know where he was. The man replied that there was a boat owner in Puerto de la Cruz who was a good friend of Wayne. His name was Captain Lopez. He described the boat and told them how to get to the wharf where it would probably be docked. He warned them that Captain Lopez was a fisherman and would probably be out fishing during the day. It was usually his habit, he went on, to leave at four in the morning and return when the sun set in the evening.

Although they were not very hungry, John and Maria ordered mero and a salad. Mero is the local sea bass, which has a mild, delicious flavor. The ensalada mixta proved to be a marvelous fresh vegetable accompaniment. This was, of course, served with the locally produced red wine.

Finishing their meal, they were surprised that they felt refreshed but not stuffed. They said goodbye to the old gentleman and drove on to the coastal town of Puerto de la Cruz where they hoped to find Captain Lopez. The directions they had been given were quite good, and they soon located the wharf where Captain Lopez and his boat, La Senora, should be.

They really didn't expect to find the boat in dock, but there it was. It was a quaint, not unattractive sloop, in need of repainting, but otherwise rather solid looking. The boat was tied firmly, and a walk ramp had been placed from the deck to the dock.

No one was in sight. After getting no answer from a number of "hellos" in both Spanish and English, John and Maria picked their way carefully up to the deck. When they got there, they looked around and tried a few more "hellos". At first there was no response, but presently a rather rough looking man opened the cabin door.

None too graciously, he growled, "What do you want?"

He spoke in Spanish, so Maria answered that they were looking for Wayne. She described her conversation with the old gentleman in the restaurant in Orotava. The captain replied somewhat shortly, "I do not know such a person." He also informed them that they had awakened him from a nap. He had been out fishing since early morning, he said, and was tired.

Strangely enough, the boat did not have the fresh fish smell that John would have expected from a boat which had recently come in with a catch. Granted, the catch could already have been loaded into trucks and taken away, but usually one would expect the odor to remain for a while.

John, who had his camera with him, asked the captain if he could take some pictures of the boat. The captain answered threateningly that he could not and asked them to leave.

As they crossed the deck, walking toward the ramp, John noticed a gold pen lying on one side, near the railing. He recognized it as being like the one Wayne had used on the plane. On the pretext of dropping a roll of film, he stooped and recovered both the film and the pen without the captain noticing.

Maria and John returned down the ramp, entered the car parked on the dock, and drove down the road with the captain scowling at them from the deck of his boat. It was obvious to both Maria and John that the man had something to hide and did not like them enquiring about Wayne.

"Our fine captain, I'm afraid, is in some way connected with Wayne's death," reasoned John. "Either he was directly responsible or knows who is."

"What are we going to do now?" demanded Maria.

"I think I will have to find out more about the captain. Perhaps when he goes out fishing tomorrow, I can question some of the other boat owners along the wharf. Then maybe later tomorrow, I can learn something more about the boat from the proprietors of some of the concessions or supply stores along the shore. Right now, however, I want to give the fine captain the impression that we are backing off and going elsewhere to take our pictures."

Only when they had driven several blocks and turned into a side street, out of sight of the vessel, did John stop. He showed Maria the pen he had recovered on the boat, and she agreed that it probably was Wayne's. She also agreed that the captain had acted suspiciously when he hadn't admitted to knowing Wayne. She felt sure the old gentleman in the restaurant had known what he was talking about when he said the captain knew him.

It was getting late in the afternoon. There was nothing more to be learned in Puerto de la Cruz unless Maria could remember other connections Wayne might have had. John asked her if she remembered any other places where people might be expected to know Wayne.

Maria reminded him that Candelaria was another village where she was sure Wayne had connections. John, however, felt that Candelaria was too far away to reach during the afternoon and still have time for any kind of investigation there today. It would be dark in several hours.

John wanted to investigate the boat further. He wanted to do so without Maria, however, as he felt it might be dangerous, given the disposition of the captain. He told Maria that he thought they had learned all they could this trip and suggested he take her back to Antonio's place. Maria protested that she would like to remain in Puerto de la Cruz overnight and do some sunbathing Sunday morning on the black sandy beaches.

John was concerned about what Antonio might think about her staying away overnight. She retorted that she had already mentioned the possibility to Nancy, and she was sure Antonio would think it proper. She was, after all, an adult. She seemed so adamant about wanting to stay that he had no choice, but he would have preferred to return Maria to Antonio's and come back to Puerto de la Cruz on his own.

Maria knew of an inexpensive hotel which was not right on the beach but close enough to walk to. While John arranged for two rooms, he insisted Maria call Antonio and tell him what they were planning to do. He cautioned her about mentioning anything about the investigation they were conducting. She promised him she would be careful. He was concerned about what Antonio might think about Maria not returning to his place tonight but guessed there was no help for it.

After they were each settled in their rooms, they walked along the beach, admired the fine black sand, and enjoyed hearing conversations in many different languages. Puerto de la Cruz is a favorite vacation spot of people from many European countries.

It wasn't until ten o'clock that they had dinner in one of the many fine restaurants bordering the beach. Maria was charming and hinted several times that she found John very attractive. She even mentioned once that sleeping alone was always so lonesome. John responded with remarks about how he missed his wife and wished she were here. He meant this. He really wished he had been more insistent about returning Maria to Antonio's place. He couldn't see himself as being attractive to young girls but apparently this one was looking for someone to take Wayne's place.

It was almost midnight when John finally persuaded Maria he was tired and needed sleep. He made a point of mentioning that he wasn't as young as she was.

Reluctantly, Maria returned to her room and John was at last free to go to his. He stayed in his room just a few minutes before going down to his car to get the blue jeans, dark t-shirt, and tennis shoes he had stashed in the back seat. He kept these for changing into for dirty work at the plant. He was sure that these dark clothes would be more suitable for his purpose than the light-colored ones he was wearing. He slipped quietly back up to his room and changed.

Leaving the hotel again, he returned to the car and drove along the coast to the wharf. He parked his bug in an out-of-the-way place where he hoped it would not be seen and recognized. He fished around for the high-powered light he had purchased in Tacoronte, tested the battery briefly, locked the car, and quietly headed out onto the wharf.

The boat was easy to locate. It didn't look as if anyone was there, but he couldn't be sure. He cautiously walked up the ramp. He didn't know what he would say if he were discovered. He had his camera with him, and he guessed he might convince some people that he wanted to take pictures of the harbor at night. He probably wouldn't be believed by anyone who knew anything about photography, but he would have to hope he met no one.

He quietly examined the entire deck of the boat and found nothing helpful. There was a bright moon, which provided the light. This was good because he certainly would not have dared use his light. He didn't want to try the front cabin door, as this would disturb anyone sleeping there.

He did find a double door in the deck leading to the cargo hold. These doors were conveniently open, so John slipped quickly and quietly below. He closed the cargo doors gently behind him and knew that if he were discovered, he would have no good explanation as to why he was there. He was just plain out of bounds.

He could smell a somewhat fishy smell in the hold, but the reason for this was obvious when he turned on his light briefly. There was a fish container over to one side. The rest of the hold was empty, except for a pile of nets up front and several empty kegs. He poked around in the nets and found a waterproof lighter underneath them. Maria had mentioned that Wayne carried a waterproof lighter. Could this one have been his?

John wondered, at this point, if Wayne had been abducted and had left a trail of his belongings intentionally, just in case someone should attempt to find him. If Maria were to acknowledge the lighter as Wayne's, along with the pen she had already recognized, Wayne's having been on this boat would certainly be confirmed. This would mean that the captain had been lying when he said he had never heard of Wayne.

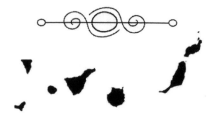

CHAPTER VIII: Trapped

Suddenly, without warning, John heard the cargo doors pushed completely shut and heard the lock bolt slip into place from the outside. He listened to footsteps retreating, heard the ramp hauled in from the dock, and knew that someone was unknotting the ropes which held the boat fast to the dock.

After another ten minutes, he heard the engines sputter and finally start. Soon he could feel the boat chugging slowly away from the wharf. He could hear no voices, so assumed the captain, or whoever was in control of the boat, was alone.

John felt pretty sure that whoever was in charge of the boat knew that he was in the hold. He couldn't be absolutely certain, however, so he didn't call out. He reasoned that if they knew he was there, it wouldn't do him any good, and if they didn't know he was there, he might have an advantage and a chance to learn something and perhaps escape later.

At first, he could hear the surf slapping against the bow of the boat and assumed the boat was headed directly out to sea. In a short while, he could sense that the boat was swinging to the right, and by the gentle roll that followed, it was fairly definite the boat was beyond the surf and headed up the coast.

He noted the time on his watch - 12:48 AM. Thank goodness for watches that could be read in the dark. He estimated they were traveling at approximately seven knots per hour. By keeping track of the time it took them to reach their destination, he might, at some future date determine where the ship was bound. Not that this information would be of any use to him at this time. He decided not to dwell on what his fate might be if the captain already knew he was in the hold, or if he were discovered later.

He ordinarily did not get seasick, but the fumes from the engine seemed as if they were being exhausted directly into the hold. The only ventilation came from the small crack between the hold doors in the deck overhead. His stomach felt queasy, and a sense of lightheadedness prevailed. He reasoned that if he could do something positive, the nauseous feeling might subside. While awaiting his destination, John busied himself feeling along the edge of the doors with his fingers.

He determined how the bolt was affixed. It seemed to be bolted on. He worked at turning the nut locks on the bolt assembly, but to no avail. They were probably rusted firmly from years of salt spray and splash. He explored the entire compartment with his hands, hoping to find either a tool for escape or one for defense. He reasoned that, if there was only one person on board to contend with, he might have a chance in hand-to-hand combat.

He came across what seemed to be a can of lubricating oil; at least that was what his nose told him. He returned to the cargo doors in the deck overhead and, using his finger, he painted some of the oil on the nuts of the door bolts - just on the off chance that, if given time to penetrate, it might make the nuts easier to get off. By keeping busy, he didn't have time to dwell on all the problems he might have to face in the near future.

Nearly an hour and a half had passed when the engine began to slow gradually and finally stopped. The sudden cessation of noise and vibration left his ears with a swishing sound. The anchor was dropped, and John listened to someone lowering what he guessed to be a small dinghy. He heard the splash as it hit the water, and then he could hear the oars slicing into the water and squeaking and thumping against the side of the dinghy, as someone rowed away. The sound became gradually fainter. John heard no indication of anyone else above deck. The most probable explanation for the departure was that the captain was going to get help from someone on shore.

This didn't exactly make sense though. The captain had seemed tough enough to deal with John on his own.

He made use of the captain's absence, if indeed it was the captain who had been piloting the boat, to turn on his light and more carefully examine the hold. Luck was with him. He found an ancient wooden tool chest affixed to the wall on the cabin side. A padlock held its door closed, but a few minutes prying with his Swiss army knife pulled the entire lock system out of the ancient wood. The chest held several saws, an array of screws, nuts and bolts, a hammer, a screwdriver, and a wrench. The hammer looked like a useful weapon and John made a mental note to take it with him, if he ever got out of the mess he was in. What really caught his attention was the wrench. He applied it to the nuts on the bolts which held the bolt plate to the hold doors. As he strained with the wrench, it seemed certain that the nuts would not give. He tried each of the nuts in turn. Finally, he was exhausted and lay back to recover his strength. He turned off his light to conserve the batteries.

All was quiet for a few minutes and then he heard a faint scratching sound, followed by two thuds, the first one sharp, and the second one soft. He knew then that he was not alone. In the next instant he felt the warmth of a warm body against him and a gentle motor-like hum. His mind was slow to assimilate this information input, probably because it was dark and he was exhausted. When his mind cleared, he realized his companion was a cat.

He stroked the animal, who curled up beside him and prepared to take a nap. John's mind became active again. He was positive the cat had not been in the hold all along. He had poked in every corner and under every net and rag. He turned on his light and crawled in the direction from which he had first heard the cat. Away from the bow of the ship, towards the cabin, the ceiling became very low, only about two feet from the floor at the furthermost point. John lay on his stomach and eased himself under the low ceiling toward the back end, or stern, of the boat. When he had almost reached the farthest point of the hold, he carefully eased himself over onto his back and turned on the lantern, pointing it upward.

Sure enough, almost directly above him, was a twelve-inch square hole, which probably opened into the galley. The cat, John surmised, was on board to discourage rats and mice from boarding the boat. The hole had most likely been put there to allow the cat free access to patrol the hold.

There was no way John could crawl through that hole, but he squirmed his way back to the main section of the hold and retrieved the wrench, hammer, and his camera. Returning to the cat's entrance, he began to hammer at the wood around the hole. He pounded with the mallet end and pried with the claw end. He gave some thought to using one of the saws, but as they were so large, he thought they would be too awkward to be effective in such a small space. Occasionally, he picked up the wrench and attacked the hole with that, just for variety. All the while, the cat watched him sleepily, probably wondering why John was going to all this bother.

After 15 minutes, by John's estimate, he was able to widen the hole enough so he thought he could crawl through. He put the tools and his camera, as well as the lantern, on the floor above. Carefully he squeezed his head and torso through the splinter infested opening. Turning on the light again, he could see that he was in what appeared to be a galley cabinet. He could see a fine crack between the cabinet doors. He pushed one of these doors gently outward and understood now why he had first heard the cat scratching. The cupboard doors were on spring hinges and the cat had probably used its claws to pull aside the door and wedge its body in. The first thud had undoubtedly been the cabinet door reclosing, and the second thud came from the cat landing in the hold.

He pushed the cabinet door open and pulled the rest of his body through the hole with great difficulty. In a very undignified manner, he managed to extricate himself from the cabinet and onto the galley floor. He arose, brushed himself off and retrieved his camera, the tools, and the lantern. He carefully brushed off the wood bits and pieces that had become attached to his clothing, swept them into a pile with his hands, gathered them up and emptied them into a nearby plastic trash bag filled to overflowing with odoriferous garbage. No point in disclosing his escape route.

He examined the cabin briefly. He didn't use his lantern as the sky was becoming light and there was a bright moon still on the horizon. He could find his way about fairly well. A quick and limited search of the cabin turned up nothing of interest. The search was not particularly thorough. His survival instinct urged John to find an immediate escape route from the boat before the captain returned, possibly with a few able-bodied thugs.

John grabbed a couple of plastic bags from a box in one of the galley cupboards, along with several wire twist-ems. He decided the bags might be waterproof enough to keep his camera from being completely ruined. A quick search showed him that there was no other dinghy on board. It seemed certain he would have to swim if he wanted to escape from the boat. He was able to locate a life preserver attached to the railing. He dislodged this and considered how he would lower himself into the water. Further investigation turned up a rope ladder hanging over the railing on the shore side of the boat. This had probably been used by the captain to climb down into the dinghy.

As he was trying to decide his next move, he heard the dinghy returning. He could not use the ladder to enter the water as he was certain that the occupant of the dinghy would see him before he could get into the water and around to the other side of the boat. He would have to exit via the anchor rope on the seaward side. Quickly he took off his shoes, stuffed them into his pockets, tucked the hammer and wrench into his t-shirt front, slipped his camera into one of the plastic garbage bags, twisted the twist-em as tightly as possible, and finally encased this bag in another plastic bag following the same procedure.

Slipping the life preserver over his head and holding the lantern and plastic bag with one hand, he was not certain that he would be able to slide down the anchor rope with his burdens. He finally removed the hammer and wrench from his t-shirt and tossed them into the ocean. He hoped the splash would be interpreted as a fish jumping. He tucked the camera into the front of his shirt, swung his legs over the rail, wrapped them around the rope, and with the lantern handle over his wrist, he grasped the rope with both hands. He slid quietly down the rope and into the water, surprised that he had made so little noise.

The water was cold, and the momentary shock left John breathless. He tried to suppress his gasps as he remained on the seaward side of the boat so as not to be seen. He could hear the dinghy approaching, and then he heard it bump against the shore side of the boat. Someone could be heard climbing the rope ladder, scraping a shoe against the side of the boat on every rope rung. When John heard the captain begin to winch up the dinghy, he quietly swam around to the shore side of the boat, pushing the life preserver in front of him. He heard the engine start and reasoned that the captain would be busy with the wheel. He paddled furiously toward the shore. He hoped the captain would not have reason to look in his direction.

He swam until he reached a rocky outcropping on the beach. Then he allowed himself to sink to a sitting position, with his back against the rocks cushioned by the life preserver. The boat he had left was almost out of sight. In fact, he could not even be sure that the speck he saw in the distance was actually the boat. John wondered what the captain would do when he discovered his prisoner was gone. He still wasn't quite sure whether or not his presence on board had been known. He had, of course, to assume that it had been. He must remember to keep an eye out for the boat in case it returned.

Marilyn Joyce Lafferty Sietsema

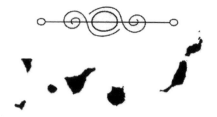

CHAPTER IX: Freedom at Last

John was physically exhausted from his swim whether
he admitted it to himself or not. He was also mentally exhausted
from the trials of his escape. He allowed himself the luxury of
sitting quietly in the shallow water and allowing the waves to
wash against him as he leaned back against a rock. When he
recovered somewhat, he decided he must explore. He wondered
where the captain had gone when he had rowed to shore. Finding
the answer to this question might shed some light on the
circumstances of Wayne's death.

It was becoming light enough so the surrounding
landscape could be clearly discerned. Perhaps John's first priority
should be to remove himself from view. If the captain had a pair
of field glasses, he might still be able to spot him amongst the
rocks, especially since the sky was lightening rapidly. Early
awaking gulls were already swooping and diving for their
breakfasts. John pulled his aching body to a crouching position
and, keeping a low profile, crawled along the shoreline for
several hundred yards until he found a pathway leading from the
sea up into the boulders that ran along behind the shore. In
places, there was a considerable expanse of beach in front of this
rocky backdrop. At other locations, the rocks extended down to
the ocean, and at some places even extended for a distance into
the water.

He followed the path he had chosen up onto the shore, to a place where the boulders completely and effectively screened him from view. Here he removed the life preserver, took his shoes out of his pockets, emptied the water from them, and set them on a rocky ledge to dry. He stripped off his jeans, wrung them out, and put them back on. He figured they would dry quickly from the breeze and his body heat when he began exploring. After doing the same with his t-shirt, he felt better. Luckily his socks were wool. When they were wrung out, he could put them back on his feet immediately, slip into his damp sneakers and not have his feet feel uncomfortable.

Upon examining his camera, he found that it had fared rather well. His flash attachment was a bit wet, but it probably would operate. His watch, which he hadn't thought to remove from his wrist, was obviously not waterproof. Droplets of water could be seen clinging to the underside of the crystal. He shook it several times but it failed to respond. All he had was a record of the approximate time he had entered the water to swim ashore. The watch was permanently stalled at 5:37. He quickly dug a hole in the sand with his hands and buried the plastic bags from view.

He climbed up the path until he reached the top of the rocky outcropping. Looking around, he noticed a dirt road a couple of hundred yards behind the rocks. It was this road that he would most likely follow when he decided to return to civilization. Hopefully, it would eventually lead to a main highway.

Meanwhile, he wanted to explore some more. He decided it would not be prudent to carry the life preserver with him, so he stowed it behind a rock, and made a mental note of its location. Turning, he retraced his steps along the path, back down to the beach. A close scrutiny of the shore showed where he had dragged himself out of the water. He wondered where the captain had come ashore.

Following the shoreline back toward what he believed was the direction of Puerto de la Cruz, he hiked perhaps half a mile. The beach became narrower, and, in some places, he had to walk through the water if he wanted to continue in the same direction. The rocks became steep cliffs, which rose higher and higher as he progressed. He could see no paths or steps which might lead to the top and hence to the road. He wondered if he would eventually have to turn about and retrace his steps if he wanted to reach the road.

As he rounded some rocks that jutted several yards into the sea, forming a rocky spur, he came upon a sheltered and scenic cove. There was a shallow beach which extended under sheer cliffs, which, at this point, overhung the beach. Someone standing on the top would not be able to see the extent of the beach below unless he lay on his stomach and looked down over the cliff.

It was here that he spotted marks where a small boat had recently landed. It had been dragged a few feet onto the beach. There was a single set of footprints leading toward the rocks and back to where the boat had been. Presumably, these were the captain's footprints. John followed these. It was with a great deal of satisfaction that he found them leading into a rock cave. John wondered if the high tide, later in the afternoon, would cover the entrance. He noticed many footprints just inside the cave, which featured a steep incline upward from the entrance. The cave seemed to become larger as he progressed and it extended quite a distance inward. It crossed his mind that this might be a Guanche cave. Then he dismissed the idea as he remembered that these early inhabitants usually located their homes in caves at higher elevations. As he advanced further into the cave, it became necessary to use his lantern when the natural light dimmed.

Upon rounding a bend in the cave, he found a multitude of wooden boxes of all sizes, piled high. There were no labels on the boxes, and they were nailed tightly shut. Straw lay scattered around on the floor of the cave and a few blades protruded from the crates. This indicated to John that the contents of the crates were fragile.

John's first thought was that here was an illegal whiskey or rum running operation. This, however, did not make much sense since there is not a tax on alcoholic beverages in the Islands. On the other hand, perhaps it was destined to be smuggled to someplace where the taxes were high. The boxes were a variety of shapes and sizes, some very large and some small.

He lifted several of the smaller ones and shook them. They gave no evidence of containing liquids. "These boxes have to contain some sort of contraband," he thought. As he advanced further along the cave, he came upon a pair of black leather dress shoes. The label indicated they were American made, size 11. He had no way of knowing or proving to himself that these were Wayne's shoes, but he suspected that they were. He would ask the Inspector General for Wayne's shoe size if he had the opportunity at a later time.

At this point, he wished he had the hammer he had dropped in the ocean. He would have liked to pry open at least one of the securely fastened lids and find out what the boxes held. He felt sure the contents of these boxes were, in some way, related to Wayne's death.

Abruptly he felt the urge to move on. Somehow, he had to find his way back to Puerto de la Cruz. His absence might send Maria to the police, and he wasn't quite ready to divulge the results of his investigation.

Before leaving, he took a few pictures of some clear footprints around the boxes and near the shoes. He included the shoes in one photograph, so that in the event they were discarded, they could still be identified later. He also photographed some of the boxes. This task completed, he left quickly. He found a fallen tree branch outside the cave and switched away his own footprints in the sand as he backed his way into the water.

He, indeed, had to retrace the path he had taken to the cove. A rock wall on the other side of the cove extended a great distance into the sea and would have been impossible to circumvent. He made most of the walk back through water, except when he went ashore briefly, several times, to erase the footprints he had previously made on the beach. He did not want to leave a message for anyone, announcing his visit to the cave.

At last, he reached the point where he had swum ashore and, after obliterating all of his footprints, he climbed carefully up the rocky path again and headed toward Puerto de la Cruz on the dirt road. He walked for several miles and finally came to a main road which led into the village of Bajamar. His watch had still shown no signs of working so he really had no good idea what time it was. He decided that his walk had dried him to the point where he looked as if he had been hiking rather than swimming.

When he reached the village, footsore and weary, he found everything closed - this was Sunday. He hailed a truck driving through the village in the direction he wanted to go. The man spoke no English, but John made him understand that he was a tourist by pointing to his camera. He pointed south and mentioned Puerto de la Cruz. The man smiled and motioned for John to climb into the seat beside him.

After several minutes, they reached the main road, which was paved and, thankfully, not so bumpy. The morning was apparently still early, judging from the light traffic. As John's stomach growled, he could not help thinking that his last meal seemed in the far distant past. As if to answer his thoughts, the driver pulled a couple of small Canary Island bananas from a paper sack and offered John one of them. John accepted this kind offer and then asked the driver, "Que hora es?" but received only a shrug in return. The man was not wearing a watch.

There were a few tourists on the road, headed for Punta del Hidelgo, no doubt. All of a sudden John's attention was drawn to a car which was approaching from the opposite direction. It looked like Archy Eaton's car. John automatically slumped in his seat. As the car passed, the driver lifted his hand in casual, friendly salute. When the car had passed, John could see it retreating in the rear-view mirror. He could see clearly enough to decide that the driver was, in all likelihood, Archy. He would like to have known if his driver was a friend of Archy's or if the greeting he had given Archy had been merely that which the driver would be likely to give to any passing motorist. He recalled that the driver had not waved to other motorists driving in the opposite direction. At any rate, John was certain Archy had not seen him. Unfortunately, he could not see whether Archy turned off for Bajamar or not. He assumed he did. He was glad that Archy had not seen him. He might have stopped and asked some embarrassing questions. John was not anxious to divulge the fact that he was still investigating Wayne's death.

He spent the remainder of the trip thinking about Archy and whether or not he had been involved in Wayne's murder. Had it been Archy who had followed him down the mountain side, the evening of the day he had discovered Wayne's body? If so, how was Archy involved? Why was Wayne killed? What was in the boxes in the cave? How was the captain involved? What had the captain delivered or retrieved from the cave? Had he been aware John was on the boat?

All these thoughts occupied John's mind as he rode back to Puerto de la Cruz. It took more than an hour for the trip.

The farmer drove right into town and began making stops at each hotel to deliver vegetables and fruits. At each stop, John helped him unload his boxes. When they finally reached the area near John's car, he pulled out his damp wallet and offered several bills to the farmer. When he refused, John did his best to thank the farmer and left him. The driver waved a friendly goodbye and went on with his deliveries. He did not seem curious about John's destination, never turning back to check where he was headed.

When John arrived back at the hotel, it was exactly 11:30 according to the clock in the lobby. He returned to his room, showered, donned his appropriate tourist clothing, and went downstairs to find something to eat. He was tired and hungry. The banana he had eaten earlier had done little to quiet his noisy stomach.

After placing his order with a waiter, he found a hotel phone, and rang Maria's room. No one answered. He enquired at the desk to see if she had left her room or had left any messages. She had left no messages, nor had she turned in her key. John began to worry but decided he needed to eat before considering anything further. While he was eating, Maria came in, wearing a bathing suit under a loose cover-up and carrying a towel. She said she had gotten up about eight and when John hadn't answered his phone, she had come down, had breakfast, and went down to the beach for some sunbathing.

John did not tell Maria of his adventure, primarily because he was afraid she might want to become more involved. He didn't think it would be safe for her to do so. She had already been of great assistance in helping him discover the captain and subsequently the cave. "I was really tired last night," he suggested. "Yesterday I had more exercise than this old decrepit body is used to on weekends."

Maria asked what was on the agenda for the day. John suggested they drive back to the wharf and take another look around. Maria agreed that they should do that and then drive east, across the Island, to Candelaria, which was on the coast on the opposite side of the Island.

John agreed, and a short time later they left the hotel, stashed the few items they had in the car and took off. If Maria noticed John's jeans and other slightly damp clothing, encased in one of the hotel's complimentary plastic laundry bags, she said nothing.

The trip out to the wharf proved fruitless as the La Senora was not in port.

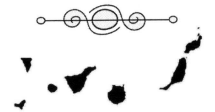

Marilyn Joyce Lafferty Sietsema

CHAPTER X: Captured

Candelaria was almost opposite Puerto de la Cruz, but it was impossible to drive directly across the island because of the mountains. It was necessary to drive back through La Victoria and Tacoronte. From there, John and Maria drove almost to La Laguna and picked up the Autopista, which took them directly to the eastern coast where they drove south to Candelaria.

Candelaria was a beautiful little village abounding in rubber trees and poinsettias. It was dominated by a large basilica, which, according to Maria, was dedicated to the patron saint of the Archipelago, Nuestra Senora de Candelaria.

Maria told John the legend about the statue of the Virgin of Candelaria. "This statue," she said, "was found on the seashore in the year 1390. It was placed in a grotto, and people worshiped it.

In the next century, Sancho de Herrera, a grandson of the conqueror of the islands, stole the statue. He took it to the eastern islands and, consequently, these islands were ravaged by a terrible epidemic. Sancho was ordered to return the statue to the grotto, only to discover that the statue was already there. This was considered a miracle."

Maria continued, "Do you believe in miracles?"

John replied firmly that he did not. He asked her where the statue was now. Maria explained that on a night in November, in 1826, an enormous tidal wave struck Candelaria, washing away the fort, its garrison and the miraculous statue.

When John mentioned that the basilica was in superb condition, Maria informed him that this was not the original building. "The original," she said, "was destroyed by fire in 1789. This new building was completed only twenty years ago." Maria added that it was here that she and Wayne had planned to be married in August.

John and Maria entered the cathedral through a side door. The interior was quiet and majestic. It seemed quite dark after the bright sunshine outside. As his eyes became accustomed to the darkness, which was broken only by the flicker of candles, John noted many beautiful religious art objects. There were a great number of statues, munificently encrusted with gold and other precious metals. Each stood in its own arched niche around the cathedral walls.

Numerous paintings hung against the stone walls, their brilliant colors in stark contrast to the cold, gray, stone background. The altar, at the front of the basilica, was a mass of carved wood, polished to a dark sheen. Overlooking the altar was a massive oil painting of the statue of the Virgin. Maria told John that this was a painting of the original statue which had been in the process of being painted when the tidal wave stuck the island. This partially finished painting was all that remained to remind the people of Candelaria of their favorite legend.

John uncapped his camera and took a picture of the painting and several of the other art objects. A young priest quietly stepped from the shadows and reprimanded him for taking pictures. He said it was not permitted. John apologized and the priest explained that picture taking was not allowed because so many original objects of great religious significance had been stolen.

He pointed to several niches that were empty. He explained that sometimes the thieves would replace an original object with a reproduction in order that the original would not be immediately missed. It was thought that photographs of the original objects were taken and used as guides in making these reproductions.

The priest could see that John was genuinely concerned and motioned for them to follow him. He led them to a back room, which was lined with old wood and glass cases, filled with intricately carved silver, gold cups, and hand-woven vestments patterned with gold thread. He told them that these objects, and many others, had belonged to the church for centuries. They had been hidden when the church was in danger of siege and rescued from fires, but alas, in the past two years many of the most valuable and important religious objects had been stolen.

This was very bad because so many of the items were used each year to celebrate certain religious holidays. They were the things that gave life to the celebrations. Shaking his head in dismay, he said he wished there were some way to bring a halt to the stealing of such treasured artifacts.

John asked the priest what was being done about the thefts. He replied that everyone in the village was commissioned to watch the items and protect them. He said that the church was guarded at all times, and that it was his opinion that insiders were, at least in part, responsible.

When they were outside the basilica again, John asked Maria if she could remember any connections Wayne might have had in Candelaria.

She thought for a moment and then responded that it may have been in Candelaria that Wayne purchased paintings. She was almost certain that an artist friend of Wayne's had lived in Candelaria. The problem was that she could not recall the man's name.

John suggested that they return to the Basilica and ask the priest if he knew of a local artist. The priest was able to assist them. He directed them to the quarters of Francis Rendez. He was the only artist that the priest knew of. He told them Sr. Rendez did not regularly attend mass but was a great admirer of church artwork. He recalled that he was especially fond of the oil paintings in the chapel and came by frequently to see them. Furthermore, the priest was able to direct them to Sr. Rendez' studio.

Maria and John drove out of the Basilica parking area and up a steep, narrow, street.

It was but a short distance to the artist's studio. This proved to be a stucco structure located on the side of the steep lane. John parked the car in front of the studio with the back wheels resting firmly against the curb and was careful to apply the parking brakes before getting out of the car.

He knocked on the door several times and they were about to return to the car when the door was slowly opened. Sr. Rendez greeted them somewhat suspiciously. John introduced himself and Maria. It was apparent that he did not feel comfortable speaking English, so John had Maria tell him that he was interested in looking at some of his paintings with an eye to purchasing several if they were to his liking.

Sr. Rendez seemed hesitant until John told Maria to tell him that he had been recommended by a friend. At this point Sr. Rendez seemed less reticent, opened the door, and urged them to come in.

The walls inside the studio were hung with multitudinous large and small paintings. The large ones had obviously been placed on the walls first, and then the smaller sized paintings were sandwiched in wherever they fit. Other canvases were leaning against the walls three or four deep.

The room smelled strongly of paint and turpentine. Several easels were in evidence, and partially squeezed tubes of oil paint were lying on top of every available horizontal surface. A few of the paintings that caught John's eyes were only partially finished. He could see that the artist liked bright, rich, colors. In evidence were a number of pictures of a religious nature. John wondered who the purchasers of these paintings were. When Maria casually asked him this question in Spanish, she reported that he told her his paintings were sold all over the world.

In halting English, he began to speak to John himself, "My art is in many churches in Europe and America. I do not only paint religious topics though. You can see I have many pictures of other things." He swept his arm expansively past all the walls of the studio. "Do you wish to buy a special subject matter? I can paint for you anything you would like."

John asked Sr. Rendez who it was that distributed his work in other countries. He didn't quite understand the question, so Maria translated. He replied that different people from different places bought his work.

John had Maria ask him if he knew Wayne Morrison. Sr. Rendez frowned when Wayne's name was mentioned and asked if John and Maria were friends of his. Maria replied that he was the one who had recommended Sr. Rendez. The artist's frown turned to a broad smile at this answer and John thought he detected a slight sigh of relief.

John asked Sr. Rendez when he had last seen Mr. Morrison. Sr. Rendez replied that he hadn't seen Wayne for more than two months. John and Maria looked around the studio, discussing the various oils and watercolors. John indicated that he was primarily interested in landscapes, and he did not see very many. Sr. Rendez showed them several partially completed canvasses of Canary Island landscapes. John was much impressed by one and told the artist that he would like to come back and look at it again when it was finished. Sr. Rendez estimated that he could complete that particular one in about a week. They said goodbye to the artist and promised that they would return in a week or so.

After they left the artist's studio, John began to think out loud, "You know Maria, I wonder if Sr. Rendez could be involved in the thefts which the priest told us about? Do you recall that he mentioned that Sr. Rendez liked to spend time looking at church paintings but never attended mass? Also, didn't the priest tell us that he could not permit people to photograph the paintings because he thought that the reproductions might be copied from photographs? I wonder if Sr. Rendez could be making those replicas of the church paintings, and if, perhaps, Wayne might have been involved. In the business he was in, it would probably not have been too difficult for him to take the original pictures out of the country after a reproduction had been substituted."

Maria appeared to be quite upset by this idea. She told John that she was positive that Wayne would not have been involved. "He may not knowingly have been involved," returned John, "but isn't it possible that he could have exported works of art which had been stolen from the church and not have realized it?"

"How could he not know if he was involved in such a practice?"

"Perhaps he thought he was purchasing copies from Sr. Rendez, when actually what he was receiving were stolen originals."

Abruptly, Maria changed the subject and said she was famished. John wanted to return to Santa Cruz but gave in and agreed to dine first at a small cafe Maria recommended. She convinced him that it was quaint and charming and warranted a quick stop. She suggested that lunch might keep his stomach from complaining out loud all the way back to Santa Cruz.

The cafe she directed him to was, indeed, quaint. It was located on a street that spoked off from the town square. To reach it, they had to descend a flight of eight steps into a dark and musty room, which was almost entirely underground.

Only the smallest amount of light was admitted from the small, grimy windows which were about a foot in height and placed just below the restaurant ceiling. John would not have agreed that the place was particularly charming. All that impressed him was the stale tobacco filled air mixed with a musty, underground odor.

Maria seemed to know the restaurant well and led him to a table. They sat down and when John's eyes became accustomed to the dim light, he could see that the cafe was more of a bar than a food establishment. True, some people seemed to be eating, but many more were sitting in groups, talking. All the other patrons were men. The only other woman was the one serving drinks. John felt uncomfortable as he noticed that the customers, who had been chatting in an animated noisy manner when they came in, were now quiet and sullen. John noticed the many furtive and suspicious glances that were cast in their direction. The waiter arrived to take their order. After their order had been taken, Maria excused herself. She returned a few minutes later and told John she wanted to show him something.

He followed her through the kitchen and down an exceptionally long flight of steep wooden stairs, into a basement. The walls of the basement were made of hand-hewn stones, fitted together without benefit of mortar. As he reached the bottom step, he could see that he was in a wine cellar. There were huge kegs lined up against one wall. He had hoped that Maria was going to lead him to another clue but there appeared to be nothing but wine kegs in this very deep, underground room.

Without warning, John was hit from behind. All he felt was a sudden surge of pressure against the back of his skull and very bright lights sparkled in front of his line of vision. He remembered this when he regained consciousness later.

When he came to, he had no thoughts at first, other than surprise that, when he opened his eyes, everything remained black. Gradually his mind became reactivated, and he was able to reiterate in his mind the events which had led to his descent on the stairs. He remembered seeing the wine kegs, and at last, he could recall the sudden bright lights after he had received the blow on his head.

Gradually, he was able to switch his thoughts to his present body position. He realized, after several minutes, that he was in a prone position on a hard, cold surface. Next, he became aware that his hands were tied. Then slowly came the recognition that his feet, too, were bound together. He noted that his mouth felt dry and rough. Then it dawned on him that he was gagged. He tried making sounds and found he could only produce some faint gurgles.

Strangely enough, he never had the impression that he was blind. His mind seemed to have comprehended instantly that he was in the dark. Even though his eyes had had adequate time to become used to the darkness, they never seemed able to penetrate it and see even the faintest outline of objects. He could see no cracks of light coming from any direction.

Feeling the floor, with his hand, he determined that it was hard packed dirt. It was a full half hour before he recalled that Maria had been directly in front of him, leading him down the stairs. What had happened to her? He still felt weak but began to explore his environment by rolling his body to the right and left, a half turn each time.

John's reasoning power was returning to its full capacity. He wanted to explore, but he didn't want to leave evidence that he had done so. If he came back reasonably close to his original prone position, each time he rolled a turn or two, he thought that his captors would not likely be aware that he had moved. Thus, he could pretend effectively that he had not regained consciousness when and if his captors did return. Rolling, instead of sliding, also made it easier to gauge his change of position in the dark, since he had no reference points.

His head began to throb. Funny; it had not hurt when he first regained consciousness. Perhaps it had hurt, but his senses were just not sufficiently alert to make him aware of the pain. From time to time his thoughts returned, in a desultory manner, to Maria. His brain registered concern for her at times, and then at other times these thoughts drifted completely away.

Several hours must have passed. During this time, John alternately moved himself about the wine cellar and returned to his original position. Sometimes after returning to his original position, he would allow himself to drift into a light sleep for a few minutes. Each time he awoke, his thoughts seemed a little clearer. As time went on, he became more and more worried about Maria. By listening and exploring, he had pretty much convinced himself that there was no one else in the cellar with him. What had happened to her?

From time to time, he discerned noises from the restaurant overhead. These were too faint to permit him to make any guesses as to what was going on up there. Recalling the great number of steps required to descend into the cellar, it did not seem irrational that one could hardly hear the sounds from the floor above. He had no accurate idea of how long he had been in the cellar nor what time it was. He couldn't twist his arm enough to see his watch. If he had been able to do so, it would have done him no good as it had stopped working sometime during the swim to shore that morning.

After what seemed like hours, the door opened at the top of the stairs. John kept his eyes closed, feigning unconsciousness, but the light emitting from above faintly penetrated his closed lids. He could hear two male voices arguing in Spanish, as footsteps descended the stairs. Then he heard a woman's voice join the argument. He sensed the voice was Maria's and was frustrated that he could not understand what she was saying. It didn't seem as if Maria's voice exhibited fear, but how could one be certain when the words could not be understood?

As the three voices came closer, he heard yet another voice from the top of the stairs. This one, too, was speaking Spanish but he recognized it as Archy Eaton's voice. What a fool he had been! Both Archy and Maria must have been involved in Wayne's death. He wasn't exactly surprised that Archy was involved, but he began to feel a sense of pain and loss of ego that he had misjudged Maria. As these last thoughts were running through his mind, he was roughly lifted from the dirt floor and carried upstairs.

As he was conveyed through the restaurant, he could hear two other voices, which he didn't think he recognized. He thought there must be at least six different people altogether. He didn't hear any dishes or cutlery being moved about or any background voices. He guessed the restaurant was closed. It was probably pretty late at night, too late perhaps, for even a late-night bar.

He heard the door open, and he felt fresh cool air as he was transported outside. The smell was definitely a night air smell, confirming his notion of the time. He was hoisted up a short flight of stairs and bundled into the back seat of a car (perhaps Archy's - he couldn't really tell). The voice of the driver sounded like Archy's. After several more minutes of conversation between Archy and the others which probably related to their destination, the car was started. The drive lasted for about an hour, first on a main road, which was relatively smooth, then along a dirt road, which produced new bruises for John every time a dip or rut was encountered. John could tell when they were going up and down hills and around curves. He figured that the last 15 minutes of the trip were spent on an unpaved road.

At last, the car came to a stop, and he was unceremoniously dragged out of the car. His whole body ached, and he incurred additional scratches and bruises as his body hit the inside of the car, the edge of the door, and finally, the rocky ground. He didn't dare indicate his feelings as he felt his chances of survival would be enhanced if the men didn't realize he was conscious.

He deduced that the car lights must be turned off as he had no sensation of lights through his closed lids. Talking was in whispers now. Some talking seemed to be in the form of questions. He could smell the ocean and hear it close at hand. He could hear the sounds his captors' feet made on the sand as they moved around him. Another car pulled up and two additional men joined the group. After further conversation and, he guessed, further decisions, he was lifted by four pairs of hands and carried down a steep path. Now, with reckless abandon, his body was even more roughly brushed against rocky outcroppings.

He sensed this might be the path he had taken when he had swum ashore. He felt, from the way he was handled, that those carrying him cared very little about his condition. This worried him because he recognized that this diabolical attitude possibly indicated that they were planning to dispose of him. His amateur investigations had apparently gotten in the way of their devious activities.

His captors carried him down to the shore and laid him on the wet sand. He feared they might be planning to drown him then and there. His fears were further substantiated when they lifted him into a dinghy. One man climbed in with him and set the oars into the water as several other individuals helped push the boat into the surf. The other occupant of the boat began to row. The rower didn't go very far from shore before he turned the dinghy to the left and rowed close to shore. John could hear the soft sounds of hikers on the shore. There were a few whispered words in Spanish, but it was easy to tell that they were purposefully being quiet. John guessed they were headed for the cave which he had discovered earlier.

After progressing in a fairly straight path for some time, the dinghy was turned toward the shore. In a few minutes, John heard and felt the scraping sound of the boat grounding itself in shallow water. He felt a tipping motion as the person who had been rowing attempted to pull the dinghy out of the water with the paddle. In another few minutes, he heard the scuffling and gruff whispers of the men who had been following them on foot along the shore. Several members of the group splashed into the water and gave the boat a final push onto the beach. They dragged his limp, sorely lacerated body out of the boat and carried him some distance before dropping him on a rough, sandy surface, against a hard rock wall. Since the surf was not as loud and he could no longer feel the sea breeze, he reasoned that he was inside some sort of shelter - probably the cave he had discovered earlier the previous morning. A light was turned on and much quiet discussion ensued. A few minutes later he could hear grunts and groans, as heavy objects were lifted and carried away.

Assuming this was the cave containing the boxes, John could only suppose that the boxes were being carried from the cave to be transported elsewhere. It would be impractical to remove the boxes by car or truck. John guessed that they were to be taken away by boat - possibly the one he had been a stowaway on. However, that boat could probably not come close enough to shore for the men to load the boxes directly aboard her. Therefore, he surmised that they would load the boxes into the dinghy and row them out to the boat. If this was their plan, it would take some time. John felt stiff and miserable and longed to move and stretch his arms and legs. He dared not do so. He conjectured that, if they thought he was unconscious, they would leave him alone. Perhaps, if the men left the cave at some time, there would be an opportunity for him to escape.

As he lay there listening to the men move about, he again wondered what was in the boxes. He thought also about what had happened to Maria, and whether or not she was a part of this gang that held him captive and seemed to think him a threat to their nefarious schemes.

After a while, the men did leave the cave and John guessed they must be rowing a load of boxes to the larger boat. He thought it probable that it was anchored in about the same spot where it had been when he had swum ashore. Before they departed, the men turned off the lantern and John was left in the dark.

John began to work on loosening the ties that held his hands behind his back. The ropes had been tied tightly and he wasn't making any immediate progress when his ears picked up a strange sound, like someone entering the cave quietly. In the next instant, he felt someone working to help him loosen the knots on his wrists. John didn't let it be known he was conscious and not a word was spoken between him and his mentor. The hands were large and firm, and John felt certain that it was a man who was releasing him. As his hands were untied, the rope was flipped aside to the cave floor. Then his unknown benefactor untied the rope holding his feet together. The man finally whispered firmly, "Keep quiet! I'm going to remove the gag. Are you alright?" It was Archy's voice.

"Yes, but I can hardly move," replied John.

"Listen carefully! I don't have time to give you any details. It will take the men no more than 45 minutes to unload and return with the dinghies. Can you walk?"

"Sure," John answered, not entirely sure he wasn't being overly optimistic.

Archy helped John to the entrance of the cave. John had, by that time recognized it as the cave he had explored earlier. Archy continued, "Ok, if you follow this shoreline," and he pointed in the direction that John was familiar with, "you will come to a steep path that leads up to your right. It may be difficult to locate in the dark, but it is the only path that will lead to the road above. The rocks bordering the beach will remain too steep to climb until you suddenly come upon a more gentle but rocky slope. This is where the path is."

John nodded, still rather dazed. Archy continued, "My car is parked on the road above the path. The keys are in the ignition. Walk back along the beach as quickly as you can. Take the car and drive to Tacoronte. Phone the Inspector General from my house. Don't lose any time. My life may depend upon your speed. I am going to simulate your body with a bundle of straw. Give me your shirt and trousers."

At any other time, John would have insisted on knowing what was going on, but Archy's request sounded honestly urgent. He would also have balked at his immodest situation, but he read the desperation in Archy's voice and realized that without Archy's help he probably would have ended up, at best, as shark food. He had the feeling that now Archy's life might depend on him, and he decided not to let him down.

Archy whispered hoarsely, "Do you think you can find your way?"

"Yes, I'm sure I can. I shall try anyway."

"Good show!"

John removed his clothing quickly and offered to assist Archy in assembling his inert replacement, but Archy insisted that he must leave immediately.

John, still feeling a bit dizzy, staggered along the beach in the now familiar path, back to where the cars were parked. He wished he had thought to apologize to Archy for having suspected him of being involved with the criminals. He made a mental note to do so later.

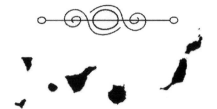

Marilyn Joyce Lafferty Sietsema

CHAPTER XI: A Fighting Chance

Still feeling groggy, John stumbled along the beach. In spite of a partial moon, it was not as easy at night as it had been the previous morning. The moon was frequently hidden behind clouds. He concentrated on remembering the outcroppings and rock spurs that he needed to circumvent. His bruised and scratched body incurred even more punishment, as he tripped and missed his footing every few steps. He stuck to his mission, sometimes staggering ahead on the sand, sometimes wading, and sometimes crawling.

He hoped Archy would remember to remove the footprints that must have remained behind when he left the cave. With a little luck, the smugglers might be fooled by the dummy Archy had constructed. As John left the cave, he had noticed that there were still many loads of boxes remaining to be transferred to the boat. He suspected they would attempt to remove everything from the cave before dawn. At last, he reached the spot where he had come ashore when he had escaped from the boat. He made his way, dripping and exhausted, up the footpath, between the rocks, to where the cars were parked.

The keys were in the ignition of Archy's car, as he had said they would be. The other cars also contained keys. John's first thought was to remove those keys in order to prevent the men from making an easy escape after the cargo in the cave was

121

removed. His second thought reminded him that Archy might need a method of escape himself. He might decide to leave while the smugglers were on their way to the boat with the last loads of goods. Also, taking the keys would not stop anyone from hot wiring the cars to get them started. The only way he could put the cars out of commission would be to alter them extensively, and that would require time - time he didn't have.

He decided to leave the keys, as they were, in the other cars and climbed into the driver's seat of Archy's car. He started the ignition and sincerely hoped that the noise of the engine wouldn't carry to the boat anchored offshore. Leaving the headlights off, he drove as fast as he dared over the bumpy dirt road. Although the night air was cool, he didn't feel cold, in spite of wearing only his underwear, wet socks, and shoes. When he reached the main road, he turned on his lights and pushed the gas pedal to the floor. The car rattled and gradually developed speed. It must have been a good twenty minutes before he reached Tacoronte. Once he was in the village, he was able to reach Archy's house in record time.

He stopped the car on the road in front of Archy's house. Giving absolutely no thought to his appearance, he jumped from the car, ran to the door of the house, and began pounding vigorously. It was only a few minutes before Archy's wife switched on a light and opened the front door. She was wearing an old bathrobe but looked wide awake. She didn't look as if she had been sleeping.

John didn't want to frighten her, but he knew that if she thought him crazy and slammed the door, it would take extra precious time for the police to arrive and be convinced of his sanity and sobriety. "Archy is in trouble!" he shouted. "We've got to contact the Inspector General. Can I use the phone?"

Apparently, it did not occur to her to question John. She stood aside and let him enter the house. She responded firmly, "I'll get the Inspector on the phone." She contacted the operator, who, in turn, must have rung the main police station in Tenerife. Someone answered the phone and a long conversation in Spanish followed. Then Mrs. Eaton held the phone, probably waiting for the Inspector to be contacted at his home. It was quite unlikely that he would be at the station at this hour. While holding the phone, Mrs. Eaton asked John where Archy was, and what had happened. This was in a matter-of-fact voice, as if she expected the unexpected from Archy.

John briefly explained that Archy was in a cave, just west of Bajamar along the coast. He told her there was not time for details, but that a gang of thieves or smugglers were loading goods on a boat, and that it was imperative that the police get there as quickly as possible if they wanted to prevent harm from coming to Archy.

Mrs. Eaton looked worried, but there was nothing John could do to put her mind at ease. While waiting for the phone conversation to be resumed, she told John he would find some dry underwear in the middle drawer of the chest in the bedroom, where she pointed. She said he would find socks in the top drawer, and that there were shirts and trousers hanging in the closet.

With an ear cocked for a resumed phone conversation, John rummaged through the indicated drawers and, indeed, found the underwear and socks. As he was taking a shirt from the closet, he heard Mrs. Eaton resume talking. Quickly he selected a well-worn bathrobe from the closet hook, threw it around himself, and returned to the kitchen and the phone conversation.

Mrs. Eaton motioned him to the phone, and upon placing the receiver to his ear, he heard the somewhat sleepy voice of the Inspector General. John briefly told him about Archy's dangerous situation. The Inspector listened carefully and then had John repeat Archy's exact location. When this had been checked once more, and he had obviously written down the explicit directions for locating Archy, he told John to drive back and meet him at the spot in the road that led to the beach. The Inspector informed him that he planned to get there as quickly as possible by car and that a police boat would come from Puerto de la Cruz. Another boat would be dispatched from Santa Cruz, but this would take longer to arrive. With no more wasted words, he hung up abruptly.

John repeated what the Inspector had said, for Archy's wife. Then he retired to the bedroom to finish dressing as quickly as possible. When he returned to the kitchen, Mrs. Eaton handed him a steaming cup of coffee. She told him there was a cup holder in the car so he could drink and drive at the same time. As he climbed into the car, she hurried around to the passenger's side and placed a sack on the seat. "Here are some cookies you can munch on while you drive." She also placed a gun beside the cookies. "It's loaded, and you may need it."

With what he hoped was a reassuring smile, he thanked her and promised to have Archy call her as soon as he was able. He started the engine, drove out of Tacoronte and back on to the main road as fast as he dared. The distance from Santa Cruz to Bajamar was a somewhat greater distance than from Tacoronte if his memory served him right. In all probability, he would arrive at the beach before the police. He had no intention of sitting there and waiting for the police to arrive before trying to help Archy. He was glad Mrs. Eaton had thought to supply him with a gun. The police would certainly recognize Archy's parked car and realize they had come to the right place.

His head still pounded, and he was sorry he had not thought to ask Mrs. Eaton for some aspirin. He was, however, grateful for the coffee and cookies. Perhaps these would help his headache and his stomach, which was beginning to feel a bit queasy.

He thought again about how glad he was that he had a gun. Arriving ahead of the police, he was pretty certain he would need it. It seemed to take him an interminably long time to return to Bajamar, although he virtually had the road to himself. He had plenty of time to worry about Archy and to wonder what had happened to Maria. He couldn't make up his mind whether she was a part of the gang involved in stealing the church treasures, or a victim of the gang, like himself. If the latter, why hadn't they brought her with them? It seemed more likely that she was involved in the scheme to smuggle something from Tenerife.

When he reached the turn-off road, he flicked off his headlights and drove once more down, what he estimated to be, the world's roughest road. He hoped Archy's tires would not blow. As he arrived at the site of the path to the beach, he noticed that the other cars were still there. He carefully parked Archy's car in the same spot where it had been originally. He left the keys in the ignition, as he had found them and, as quietly as possible, slipped down the footpath to the water, and struggled back along the shoreline. At one point he removed his sodden shoes, tied them together, and slung them over his shoulder. He felt he could move more quickly and quietly without them.

He had been along this shore so many times in the last 24 hours that he felt as if he knew every blinking rock and pothole from personal encounter. How had he gotten himself into this mess? Still, he couldn't complain about lack of excitement. He vowed to lead a quiet unconcerned life and never become involved in investigating again if this caper turned out positively. If he could just reach the cave in time to keep Archy from bearing the brunt of his bungling.

As he stealthily approached the cave site, he could hear a conversation in Spanish carried on in whispered tones. He could detect great activity but could, so far, discern no agitation. Could it be possible that they had not, as yet, discovered his absence?

Before slipping around the last rock outcropping, he looked up to see if there were some way he could view the cave entrance without actually going around that last rocky spur, which extended 100 feet or so into the sea. If he got to the end of the spur, he could readily be seen by anyone approaching in a dinghy from the sea. He could discover no footholds along the beach. There was nothing but steep rock walls. Finally, he decided to sit tight and wait. As long as he heard no agitation, he could probably assume his absence had not been discovered and that Archy was still safe. If he did hear something to suggest otherwise, he could reach the cave quickly and use his gun, if necessary.

He continued to hear sounds of lifting and loading for the next 10 minutes or so. Then he heard a loud shout. If he could only understand Spanish! He vowed to take a crash course if he survived this adventure. He heard what sounded like arguing. Voices were no longer the whispers they had been. Now was the time to move. He decided to risk it and see what was happening. He entered the water and edged his way along the rock spur, making virtually no noise.

Meanwhile, the shouting and arguing continued at the cave site. As he peered over the first rock that was sufficiently low, he could see Archy by lantern light. Three burley looking characters surrounded him. As John watched, one of the characters grabbed Archy by his shirt front with one hand and socked him in the jaw with the other fist. Archy collapsed and one of the other men viciously gave him a tremendous kick in his side. Almost simultaneously, a third man pulled a gun from his pocket, aimed it at Archy's head and cocked it. At this point, the man who had knocked Archy down shouted a string of curses, and in no uncertain terms told the holder of the gun to put it down. The ruffian, obviously respectful of this man who was issuing the orders, let his arm fall to his side with the gun pointing harmlessly toward the ground.

At a subsequent order, one of the men retreated into the cave and came out bearing the ropes that had bound John several hours earlier. The three men tied Archy's hands and feet and rolled him roughly against a rock wall on the other side of the cove. It looked as if John's escape had been discovered, and the blame was being placed on Archy.

Meanwhile, the dinghy was returning from the boat empty, after having transferred its load to the ship anchored offshore. There were not more than fifteen or twenty boxes left to transport. John calculated that the dinghy had returned for the last load. As the two men in the dinghy pulled the boat to shore, the three men who had overcome Archy rushed to the tiny boat. Although John could not decipher their words, he was sure they were telling the new arrivals about Archy.

One of the men from the dinghy, pulled his gun from its holster and climbed onto the sand, heading in Archy's direction. The other grabbed the first man's arm and shouted something in Spanish that must have included some fiery obscenities. He, in turn, drew a knife from his pocket and stomped toward Archy.

John could endure it no longer. He stepped over the last fringe of protruding rock, splashed toward the shore, pointed the gun in the direction of the five men and yelled, "Stop!" One of the characters on the beach quickly pulled a gun and fired a shot at John. He had not aimed carefully enough, and John sidestepped the shot and shot the gun out of the man's hand, before he could get off another shot. The man yelled in anguish and John guessed the bullet had struck his hand from the way he was holding it and dancing about. Another of the toughs reached for his gun but dropped it almost immediately as John shot him in the leg. This sent the man tumbling to the ground holding his leg and shouting what John took to be additional oaths.

John shouted for the nearest man to untie Archy before he got the same treatment. The man looked at John blankly and John suddenly realized that he could understand only Spanish. From the heap of humanity, hog-tied against the far wall, John heard his commands translated into Spanish by Archy, with a few added invectives, he suspected. Immediately, the smuggler hurried to Archy and untied his bonds with great difficulty - probably because he was hurrying, in an attempt to forestall the same treatment John had afforded his companions.

Archy staggered to his feet and, with a smile on his face, called to John, "Just in time, Matey!" Archy told the remaining three men to drop their guns and knives behind them and to put both hands over their heads. He gathered all the weapons and stashed them in all his available pockets, except for one gun, which he cocked and held ready in his hand. He handed another gun to John, "Just in case the one you have jams! Keep them covered while I get some rope." Archy gathered up the ropes that had bound John and himself and then ducked into the cave entrance.

Moments later, he returned from the cave with some additional rope. He began to cut these into suitable lengths. He ordered the nearest man to lower his hands and cross them behind his back. After tying his hands, he asked him if he wanted his feet tied in a standing or sitting position. The man answered by lowering his body to the sand.

John recognized the next thug Archy tied as the restaurant owner from Candelaria. John asked Archy to inquire as to why they had taken him captive at the restaurant. Archy discussed the matter in Spanish, as he continued tying. In a few minutes, he reported, "He says you know too much." This confirmed John's suspicion that Maria was in some way connected with his own kidnapping. He remembered too that it was after he had shown an interest in the paintings that had been stolen from the Basilica, that Maria had looked at him questioningly. It was easy now to make the connection between those same stolen church paintings and artifacts and the crates in the cave. It seemed possible that Maria might even have been involved in Wayne's death in spite of her professed love for him.

129

John had Archy ask the same man where Maria was. He responded that he didn't know any Maria. John asked Archy to remind him that she had been with him in the restaurant. The man continued to insist that he had not known the girl. Archy pushed his gun into the man's stomach, but he insisted that he did not know what had happened to the girl.

John explained to Archy that this could not be true, as he had heard the girl's voice in the restaurant when he was being carried to the car.

"These fellows will stick to a story, even though they know you know they are lying," responded Archy.

Before John could have Archy question the man further, another dinghy paddled quietly into view. John knew that there had not been another dinghy aboard the boat he had been a stowaway on, so he wondered where this rowboat had come from. Another dinghy may have been added to speed the transportation of the crates from the beach to the boat. Apparently, the men aboard the boat had observed what had taken place on shore. They may even have used binoculars. At any rate, they approached the shore with guns aimed and ready to fire. Even before the boat was beached, the men in it began firing at Archy and John.

Archy quickly grabbed the two lanterns and doused them. What followed was a free-for-all. The moon was hidden behind a cloud bank, so there was practically no light. Shots were fired but did not often meet their marks. John could hear one of the remaining untied prisoners scream in agony as a shot, fired from the arriving crewmen, hit him by mistake.

John, realizing the futility of wasting shots, and possibly killing or injuring someone accidentally, flattened himself in the sand behind a rock. He kept ever alert, with his gun ready to fire in case the moon came out from behind the clouds, or in the event someone managed to find and light a lantern.

The wild firing continued for what seemed like an unnecessarily long time but was probably over in only a few minutes. At last, a motorboat could be heard approaching from the seaward side. It was without lights. John hoped this was the police and not more assistance for the criminals. His hopes were answered when a powerful headlight was turned on and instructions were issued over an electrically powered megaphone.

Some of the smugglers ran into the cave. Others started toward the sea and into the water, in an attempt to get around the outcropped rock and to the safety of the beach beyond. This was, of course, an impossible task, with the police in the way. A few shots were fired, but the fighting was quickly over.

As the police boat hit the shore and came to a grinding halt, at least a dozen uniformed officers leapt from the boat. The policemen switched on additional individual lanterns and the smugglers threw their guns to the ground, raising their hands high above their heads. They were soon rounded up into a small cluster, their guns collected, and their hands handcuffed behind their backs.

Just as a lantern moved in his direction, searching for additional criminals, John rose stiffly from behind his rock and was greeted by a bright light shining directly in his eyes, and a sharp order in Spanish, which he guessed to be an order to drop his gun. He did so, and for added safety, raised his hands.

At this point, he heard Archy shout to the policeman. He put his hands down only after the policeman came closer, apologized, and indicated, with a smile, that he could lower his arms. By this time, police sirens could be heard approaching on the road above, and John was surprised to hear them screech to a halt directly above the cove. He was even more amazed, in the next few minutes, to see policemen lowering themselves on ropes, down into the cove.

From the sea, a second police boat, with heavy search beams could be seen alongside La Senora. Policemen were boarding the boat with grappling hooks and rope ladders. A few shots were fired by the smugglers and then all was quiet.

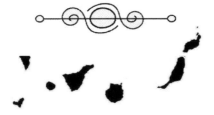

CHAPTER XII: Surprise Finding

The policemen distributed all the smugglers, more or less evenly, among the many police cars they had brought to the site. They were taken to the jail in Santa Cruz. Archy remarked that they might not have room there for all the prisoners and might eventually have to take some of them to the jail at Puerto de la Cruz.

One of the police boats returned to Puerto de la Cruz, followed by the smugglers' boat which was piloted by a police captain. Archy and John remained at the cave site along with the other police boat. Several policemen scouted up as many lanterns as they could muster from the boat and set out to search the cave interior thoroughly.

By this time, John didn't need Archy to tell him what was in the boxes that had been stored in the cave by the smugglers. As he had theorized, the men that had just been taken prisoner were connected with the many thefts of church artifacts. There were only a few packed boxes remaining, as almost all of them had been loaded aboard the smugglers' boat. However, with the help of several of the police boat crew and a good crowbar, John and Archy opened the remaining boxes. These contained, without exception, objects that belonged rightfully to churches on the Island. There were well executed statues of virgins, covered artistically with gold leaf, hammered silver chalices.

133

meticulously embroidered alter clothes, and other exceptionally beautiful artifacts. These were carefully repacked and loaded aboard the police boat. According to the police captain, all the articles which had been confiscated from the crooks would be checked against a list of missing objects at headquarters. They would be held in the police vault until the men were brought up for trial. The articles would be used as evidence during the trial, after which they would be returned to their rightful owners.

After the cave had been thoroughly checked, one of the policemen asked John and Archy if they wanted to return to headquarters with them in the boat. Archy declined, indicating that he had his car parked on the road above the beach. "One thing you can do for me," requested Archy, "Contact my wife and let her know that I'm all right."

"I'll use the radio phone as soon as I'm back on board," replied one of the policemen.

"Do you want us to take you around to the beach where your car is parked? It will just take a few minutes by boat," called another.

"No," replied Archy, "I think we'll examine the cave a bit more. I don't mind getting wet and John here is already soaked."

The dinghy from the police boat left, leaving Archy and John with a couple of lanterns and a shovel - in case Archy's car got stuck in sand or mud on the old dirt road. Archy and John set about examining the cave once more. They started from the front of the cave, using a lantern and the shovel to carefully examine every nook and cranny. Early on, they discovered several pieces of silver, one jewel, and other odds and ends which had apparently fallen from artifacts carelessly handled by the smugglers. This is what one would expect, thought John.

It took several hours to complete the task. They had almost decided to look no further when they got to a point in the rear of the cave where they could see no more footprints. They were tired and it was fairly evident that the smugglers had not gone beyond this point. However, John was curious. "This cave still goes back quite a way," he told Archy. "As long as we have these bright lanterns, let's at least give a superficial glance at what lies beyond."

Archy too, was an adventurer at heart. They worked their way back an additional several hundred yards and found nothing of interest beyond the unusual structure of the cave. John decided that the cave was probably never under water except, perhaps, during a very bad storm. This was evidenced by the fact that the boxes containing the artifacts had shown no signs of being wet. It was also evident that some of the boxes had been in the cave for quite some time. There were spiders, wasps, and other insects galore, who had made the boxes their permanent homes.

As they reached a point in the cave where the ceiling slanted downward sharply, leaving little room for further investigation, they decided to quit their explorations.

Just at this point, John noticed what appeared to be a rusty metal object protruding from the sand floor at a point where the cave roof almost touched the floor. Archy and John took turns, holding the lantern and using the shovel to remove some of the sand from around the object. As more and more of the sand was removed, it appeared that some sort of statue was concealed beneath the remainder of the sand. The protrusion they had discovered was the arm. The statue appeared to be about life size and to be lying on its side. They continued to dig, their fatigue vanishing with the excitement of their discovery.

After an hour and a half of concentrated digging, brushing sand away, and lifting carefully, they managed to free the object. The statue was obviously of some special religious significance. "I wonder," said Archy, "why the smugglers put this one back here? Perhaps one of the men wanted to keep it for himself. Probably thought he could come back at some later date and dig this out and sell it on his own. It doesn't surprise me that one crook would try to cheat his fellow crooks. It's just instinctive for them, I guess."

They carefully dragged the statue back across the sand, using Archy's jacket under the statue, so as not to damage it. When they reached the beach, they continued to drag it until they had it at the water's edge. Then they scooped handfuls of water over the statue until they had most of the sand removed from its surface. When they examined it closely with the lantern, John could not believe his eyes. It looked exactly like the picture he had seen in the cathedral at Candelaria. He also recalled that the original statue had been swept into the sea during a tidal wave. Was it possible that this was the lost statue? It did show evidence of having spent a long time in the cave. There were pock marks, and much of the paint was chipped, but it had at one time possibly been a work of art.

Both men were excited. Although Archy was not familiar with the Virgin of Candelaria, he could see that this statue was an antique. The problem was going to be how to transport the darn thing. They certainly could not drag it around

the rock spur and up the beach and then up the footpath to
Archy's car.

It was determined that one of them would have to
remain at the site while the other went for assistance. They
thought that perhaps the police boat could be returned to rescue
the stone lady. Archy volunteered to remain with the statue while
John drove to Bajamar to phone the police at Puerto de la Cruz.
John reached Bajamar without incident and put in the call. The
police said they would start back with the police boat. John didn't
tell them the significance of the artifact they had found. He did
explain about the size, and they felt certain they had a crate from
one of the other treasures that could be used.

John returned to the beach to keep Archy company until
the police boat arrived. As they sat on the beach, the two men
had much to talk about.

Marilyn Joyce Lafferty Sietsema

CHAPTER XIII: Explanations

Archy explained to John that he was an undercover agent for the Spanish authorities. He had actually been an international investigator for the British government before his retirement. The Spanish government had hired him after his retirement, partly because of his credentials, and partly because of his ability to pose as a retired government worker. There were many retired British government workers living on Tenerife.

His knowledge of Spanish enabled him to get to know the local population and, finally, the local smugglers. It had been known to the authorities for a number of years that articles of great value were being smuggled out of the Islands. They were appearing in the museums of other countries and in private collections. In the past few years, the rate of articles being smuggled out of the country seemed to have increased rapidly. The Spanish authorities decided that something needed to be done or they might eventually lose many of their national treasures.

Archy spent several years making friends among the local people before he was approached. He had lived in Tacoronte for the past three years, and only in the past six months had he made contact with the smugglers. "Most of the people in the Islands are good people. They have great respect for the property of the church and other people. In fact, most of

139

them are devout Catholics and would give their own lives to protect church property. They feel that the church belongs to them."

For all practical purposes, Archy had become one of the smugglers, as far as they were concerned. He laughed when he mentioned that he had helped engineer some of the heists. This was the only way he could incorporate himself into the heart of the organization. His job was to discover who the leaders were and how the artifacts were disposed of. It was thought that the organization was international, as similar problems had been developing on the Spanish mainland. As a matter of fact, some of the authorities thought that the smuggling ring probably extended over the entire European Continent.

Unfortunately, although he had been working with the operation for more than six months, he had not discovered where the materials were being shipped or who was responsible for running the operation. He was afraid that now that his cover had been blown, work would have to start over on trying to locate the leaders, and he would not be the one who could do it.

John told Archy about the pictures he had taken of the footprints in the cave where Wayne's body was found. He told him that he had also taken photos of several tire tracks and prints which he had found in the sight-seeing area, directly across the road from the cave. John explained that he had mailed the film to the United States and that it should be coming back soon. Archy was very interested and seemed pleased with this. He thought that it might help convict some of the local men who were involved. The operation would at least be stemmed in Tenerife for a while.

John could not refrain from asking Archy if he was the one who had followed him down from Tacoronte the evening of the day Wayne's body was discovered. Archy assured John that it had not been him. "The next day," Archy continued, "a very careful search was made of the cave and the area around it. The Inspector General assigned six men to the task. I recall that afterwards he was concerned because there were so few prints in the cave, considering there had been so many of us in there. Apparently, the fellow who returned to the cave after you, did an outstanding job of eradicating the footprints. Your photographs will certainly be of great interest to the Inspector General."

John listened with amazement and then asked Archy if he knew what part Wayne had played in the operation. "You've got me there," replied Archy. "The first time I saw the bloke was there in the cave. I examined his body in my wine cellar. Unfortunately, I didn't uncover any pertinent information."

At Archy's request, John explained again about his meeting Wayne on the airplane, about his seeming disappearance at the airport in Madrid, and about his reappearance at the hotel. He also disclosed the information he had obtained from the room clerk at the Mencey. He told Archy that he was just about certain that the man named William Morton, who had disappeared from his room at the hotel, was Wayne Morrison. Archy agreed that it seemed likely. He thought that the first thing they would need to do was to suggest to the Inspector General that the luggage which Morton, or Morrison, had left at the hotel be examined.

John reiterated how he had discovered that his secretary had known Wayne. He had thought at the time that this was a stroke of good luck. Now he wondered if perhaps he had been set up. On looking back, he thought it was possible that Maria had been placed in her position to find out what he knew about the smuggling operation. John told Archy to remind him to question Antonio and Guillermo about how they had located and hired Maria. Why she had given John as much information as she had about Wayne's activities in Tenerife was a question neither of them could answer. One thing that seemed plausible was that she had, at some point, decided that John knew more than he should. There was merit to the theory that it wasn't until John had shown interest in the art that had been stolen from the basilica in Candelaria that Maria thought he knew more than he really did and made the decision to lead John to the smugglers so they could get him out of the way. According to this theory, it was possible that John's meeting Maria was just a coincidence. If Maria could be located, she might be able to clear up this point. She had, after all, given John accurate information about Wayne's address in New York.

Archy seemed elated when John told him that Irene had already done some investigating in New York concerning Wayne. He nodded his head, in appreciation, when John said that Wayne's company was World Wide Import-Export. Perhaps Wayne had been an unsuspecting ally of the smugglers. After all, if his business was importing unique objects for sale, perhaps he unknowingly was helping the smugglers distribute their merchandise. Maybe he was killed because he discovered the true nature of the artifacts he was importing and threatened to go to the authorities.

John continued by describing his drive with Maria to La Victoria on Saturday. He told him about their visit to the potter's house: "Maria seemed eager to help discover how Wayne met his death. After we had purchased a few ceramic containers and learned nothing of importance from the old lady who was working there, we drove on, and had lunch in a restaurant in La Orotava where Maria was certain that Wayne was known. The owner recognized Maria and seemed surprised that she was not with Wayne. He knew nothing of Wayne's whereabouts but directed us to the captain of the La Senora, a boat docked in Puerto de la Cruz. He told us the captain was a good friend of Wayne's. We located the captain, but he was distinctly unfriendly when I questioned him about Wayne. As I was leaving the boat, I discovered an American gold pen on the deck. It looked like one I had seen Wayne use. It could, of course, have belonged to someone else. It didn't seem like the sort of item the captain would own, however. I was able to pick up the pen without being noticed when I dropped a roll of film. It seemed to me, at the time, that the captain would have had to be involved with Wayne's death in some way."

"Maria and I decided to spend Saturday night in Puerto de la Cruz," John continued. "Later that night when Maria and I were established in our rooms, I snuck out, with the idea of looking over La Senora more thoroughly, to see if I could discover any additional clues."

John told Archy how he had stayed aboard La Senora too long and had become an inadvertent stowaway. He detailed his escape, and how he had located the cave and photographed the boxes and shoes that he thought might have been Wayne's.

Archy recalled that Wayne's body had been found without shoes. John went on to describe how he hitched a ride back to Puerto de la Cruz Sunday morning. Archy informed John that it was him he had passed when he was being driven to Puerto de la Cruz. The gang members living in Bajamar had called a meeting there Sunday morning.

John told Archy about driving to Candelaria, where Maria had told him she and Wayne had planned to be married. She had thought John should see the Cathedral there. He then went into detail about his discussion with the priest at the cathedral concerning stolen church artifacts. It was here too, that he learned the legend of the statue of the Virgin of Candelaria from Maria. "You know," said John, "if this statue turns out to be the long-lost Virgin of Candelaria, it will be a fringe benefit of the investigation."

Archy agreed and suggested further that the people of the area would probably want to turn the event into a big celebration.

John completed his story with the episode where he was taken captive in the basement of the restaurant in Candelaria. He described how Maria had insisted that they have dinner at that restaurant, before returning to Santa Cruz.

At this point, Archy took over and told what had happened upstairs, while John was bound and gagged in the cellar. "I was back in Tacoronte spending a quiet Sunday afternoon with my wife, when I received a phone call from Louis, the restaurant owner in Candelaria. He said there was a problem, and for me to round up the rest of the lads and drive to the restaurant, as quickly as possible. When we got there, he told me about you. I wasn't given much explanation as to why they had taken you prisoner. They seemed to think it would be absolutely necessary to put you down. I tried to convince them it would be safer for the operation to hold you until all the boxes were removed from the cave and shipped away. Maria was there too -- that was the first time I had seen her. I assumed, from her Spanish conversation, that she was Spanish. Her dialect was different from the local dialect, but this might have meant she was from the mainland. I hoped, at the time, that she might be a link to the brains behind the smuggling operation."

Archy explained that Maria had agreed with him, that John should not meet with an accident. She suggested that because you were an American, it would be unwise to kill you. She said your death might draw attention and result in an investigation by international authorities. "Even though she was responsible for leading you into the restaurant," explained Archy, "she was not in favor of killing you. She did feel that you should be kept captive and under sedation until the current operation was complete. The men were adamant, and I finally had to go along with their scheme to load the merchandise and then dispose of you. I knew I would have to figure out some way to keep you alive."

John remembered that he had been carrying his camera and flash unit with him when he descended into the wine cellar. He asked Archy if he knew what might have happened to them.

Archy recalled seeing Maria carrying a camera bag when he first met her at the restaurant. "While we were carrying you unconscious from the basement, Maria probably put them in your rented car. I don't think the VW was still parked in front of the restaurant when we lifted you into my car, so she must have driven away by then."

"Fortunately," replied John, "I had put my latest exposed roll in a mailer and left it at the desk of the hotel in Puerto de la Cruz, to be picked up by the mailman. That was before I left with Maria to drive to Candelaria this morning. That was the roll that contained the pictures of the boxes in this cave, some shots of footprints here in the cave, and the picture of the shoes that might be Wayne's. Those shoes don't seem to be around now. You didn't notice if one of the officers found them, did you?"

Archy answered that he had not noticed them. He speculated that they were probably out in the ocean somewhere, by now.

At this instant, the men could hear the police boat returning. It was a good-natured group of officers that rowed ashore with materials with which to pack the Virgin of Candelaria.

"What have we here? A little loot we forgot to take?" yelled one of the men.

"No," answered Archy, "We think this might be the statue of the Virgin of Candelaria that was supposedly washed out to sea by a tidal wave in the early 19th century."

"I'll be damned!" muttered the officer. "Where did you find her?"

"In the cave. We wanted to make sure there were no further clues, so we explored the cave to the point where the roof of the cave slopes down to the ground. It was there that we saw part of the statue protruding from the sand. At first, we thought it was part of the cache of the smugglers, but it was too deeply imbedded. It took us awhile to dig her out. It's a good job you left us with a shovel."

"Well, we'll take good care of the lady. She looks as if she has been leading a hard life. She could use a little renovating."

The policemen carefully wrapped the statue in blankets, fashioned a rough crate from some boards they had in the dinghy, and hauled the virgin aboard. They waved as they rowed out to the police boat. Archy and John were free to trek back to Archy's car. Tired as they were, both men sighed when they finally reached the car and climbed in.

Dawn had arrived, and the sky was light when they reached Archy's house. Archy's wife greeted them warmly and gave them welcome mugs of hot coffee. She offered to prepare a good breakfast for them. It was at this moment that they both realized that neither of them had eaten dinner Sunday evening. John also recognized that it was Monday morning, and he would be expected at work. They both were glad of the opportunity to change their wet clothes. John's clothes had been dried and pressed by Archy's most considerate wife.

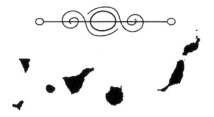

Marilyn Joyce Lafferty Sietsema

CHAPTER XIV: Back to Work

John called the Amco factory as soon as they were open. After telling Antonio about his weekend adventures, he asked if Maria had come to work. Antonio replied that she had not come in yet, nor had she phoned. Antonio suggested that John take the day off and catch up on his sleep. John declined the well-meant offer and said he would be in as soon as he could get back to the hotel, change into another outfit, and see about renting a second car. He also planned to alert the police to the disappearance of his VW. He wanted to call Irene and let her know he was all right. She had been expecting a call from him Sunday evening and might be worried. Antonio said he would contact Irene right away and that John could talk to her again later.

Archy then used the phone to talk to the Inspector General. He arranged to see both Archy and John later in the afternoon for a statement. "He seemed most pleased with the number of crooks that were caught - 13 in all," said Archy.

Archy and John sat down to a delicious breakfast. Between bites, Archy again described everything that had happened for the benefit of his wife. They all wondered if any of the 13 men who were in jail would reveal enough information to indicate who their leader was. Archy wasn't sure. He said they might remain quiet, out of fear of reprisals to their families.

"Who do you think heads up the group?" John asked Archy.

"It's difficult to tell. I would guess that it has to be someone who has outside connections for disposing of the stolen articles."

"Could it have been Wayne? He certainly had the means for distributing artifacts," suggested John.

"He may have been part of the organization - even an important part - but I doubt he was in charge. If he had been, his death would probably have brought about a cessation of the operation, at least temporarily. That didn't happen. Indeed, his death may have been brought about by his inquisitiveness concerning the operation."

"Isn't it possible, though," interjected John, "that Wayne was doing so well, that someone else wanted a piece of the action, so to speak? Perhaps he was killed because someone else wanted to take over the smuggling organization and make the profit themselves."

"That is one possible explanation," replied Archy.

With breakfast over, Archy drove John back to his hotel. When John reached his room, he removed his clothes, dumped them on the bed, and headed for the shower. After drying, he looked in his closet for something comfortable to wear. It suddenly dawned on him that his clothes were not in the same order in which he had left them. Further examination convinced him that his underwear was in a different location in the chest of drawers. After looking in his briefcase, he decided that his working papers were not in the same order either. It looked as if someone had searched his room over the weekend.

After dressing, John called the desk and asked to talk to the maid who had serviced his room on Saturday and Sunday. The clerk told him that the same girl had made up his room on both days. When John asked if he could talk to her, the room clerk responded that she was probably on duty now, cleaning the rooms on his floor.

John requested that the clerk come up for a few moments and translate for him. He told the clerk he had a few questions to ask the maid. The room clerk assured John that the maid was an honest Guanche girl who had been working for the hotel for several years. John replied that he did not think anything was missing. He just wanted to ask her a few questions.

The clerk, rather puzzled, met John at the door of his room and they located the girl. She accompanied them to John's room. When he asked what condition his room had been in on Saturday morning when she came to clean, she replied that it had been in a normal condition.

"On Sunday morning," she offered, "your room was a mess! The drawers were open, your clothes were all over the bed and floor, and the papers from your briefcase were dumped in the middle of the carpet. It looked as if a storm had blown through. I cleaned and straightened everything as best I could. Perhaps some of your suits and trousers will need pressing."

John asked her if she had reported the mess to her superior. She answered that she had not. She had figured that he might have gotten drunk on Saturday night and made the mess himself. After a brief Spanish conversation with the clerk, she told John that she had taken nothing, only put things back where she thought they might belong.

John assured the maid that he did not suspect her of taking anything and that, in fact, he didn't think anything was missing. He did ask her if she had seen anyone lingering in the halls Sunday morning when she came to clean. She recalled only one older gentleman coming down that hall. She had not seen him before, but he did not look like he would be a thief.

The clerk returned to his desk in the lobby with John and checked the guest list. There were several older gentlemen registered in rooms on John's floor. The one the maid had seen might be any one of them or it could have been someone who was not even staying at the hotel. John thanked the clerk and tipped him. Before he returned to his room, he located the maid again and gave her an especially generous tip.

John decided to put in a call to Irene. It was 10:30 Tenerife time. This meant it was 3:30 a.m. in New York. He called anyway, knowing Irene was one of those rare sleepers, who can wake up, carry on a stimulating conversation, and go right back to sleep afterwards.

He placed the call, and it went through almost immediately. There were not many calls going to New York at that time. Irene was happy to hear his voice. She told him Antonio had called an hour ago and filled her in on as many of the details as he knew.

John, knowing Irene so well, could feel a sense of excitement in her voice, so he let her continue. "I picked up the cosmetics Wayne's mother had ordered from Clara about nine o'clock Saturday morning. I decided to deliver them to Wayne's apartment address where Mrs. Schumacher lived. I called first, which is the custom, according to Clara. She said that it is always a good idea to deliver goods as soon as possible and to always call first, before making a delivery. She said this saves a lot of time and avoids trying to make deliveries when people are not home."

Irene continued, "Mrs. Schumacher was home and told me she would be there all day so to bring her purchases over anytime. The problem was that when I arrived, about ten o'clock, and rang the doorbell, no one answered. I persisted, but still got no response. Finally, I rang the bell of the apartment manager. She said she had not seen Mrs. Schumacher go out, but then, she had been down in the basement, washing. In view of the fact that Mrs. Schumacher had made an appointment, we both agreed that a check should be made to make sure she was not ill. The manager took her keys, and we went up to her apartment. Several vigorous knocks brought no response, so she unlocked the door."

"You can't imagine the mess we encountered. Everything seemed to be turned over, out of place, or smashed. All the drawers in the apartment seemed to be out, with their contents on the floor. Even the flour and sugar canisters in the kitchen were emptied onto the counters. We found Mrs. Schumacher in the bedroom, dead, apparently from a heavy blow to her skull."

"We called the police, of course. I didn't disclose anything about my investigation of Mrs. Schumacher. I just showed them my credentials from Clara, and they assumed that I was selling cosmetics to earn additional money."

"I hate to consider what might have happened to you if you had decided to arrive earlier," John went on to say, and added, "I shall have to report what has happened there, to the Inspector General here. He will, undoubtedly, make contact with the New York Police. I imagine they will work together on the case. Meanwhile, you need to be very careful dear. I don't suppose a connection will be made between you and the investigation of this case but do take every precaution. It might not be a bad idea to move in with Clara for a while."

"Clara suggested that too," answered Irene. "It is probably rather unlikely that anyone would connect your interference in the smuggling operation there, with my nosing around here, but it will be fun to stay with Clara anyway. I shall accept her invitation and move in with her tomorrow morning." She also told John that she had checked with the photo processors and that the duplicate negatives and pictures were on their way. "I expect the other set to be in my mailbox today or tomorrow," she said. "I shall take them with me to work and put them in our safe as soon as they arrive. Clara will watch for them while I am at work."

"Sounds great!" replied John. "I sent another roll of film off Sunday, so you may want to follow the same procedure with this one. Take care! I love you, and miss you!" When John hung up the phone, he still felt worried about Irene, although he realized she was intelligent and quite capable of taking care of herself.

When John arrived at the rental agency to rent another car and explain about the first one, the manager informed him that he had found John's car parked in front of the agency when he arrived that morning. John explained that the car had been taken late Sunday afternoon. They both examined the car. It seemed in good shape. To John's surprise and delight, when he opened the trunk he found his camera bag there, complete with all his equipment: camera, flash unit, and tripod. He examined the camera and it seemed to be in good condition. Even the film was still intact. He recalled, however, that Maria had watched him load film into his camera when they arrived in Candelaria. She had been present when he took pictures of the cathedral and town. She would have known that the film contained nothing incriminating.

At any rate, he was glad to have his camera back and drove happily toward the industrial area of Santa Cruz. When he arrived at the Amco Plant, Antonio informed him that he still had not heard from Maria. John reiterated all the events of the past weekend for both Antonio and Guillermo before they got down to business.

At three o'clock, John left the plant and drove to police headquarters. There, Inspector General de Lucas greeted him and invited him into his office. Archy was already there waiting. They went over all the events in detail while another young officer took notes. Every once in a while, the Inspector General would interject a question to clarify a particular point. Mainly he listened, twisting the tip of his moustache between his thumb and forefinger.

John brought them both up to date on what had happened in New York and his wife's part in the happenings there. The Inspector General put in a call to New York. When the call came through, he discussed the case at length with the American inspector on the other end of the line.

The sum and substance of the call was that the New York Police had no clues as to the assassin or assassins who had murdered Mrs. Schumacher. The police were conducting an investigation in the immediate neighborhood to determine if anyone had observed strangers entering the apartment at the time they suspected the old lady may have been murdered. They had been able to pinpoint the time of death quite accurately. They knew that the old lady must have been killed between the time Irene phoned her and the time when Irene and the landlady discovered the body.

The New York Police said they would be talking to Irene later in the day, to get more details directly from her. They agreed to investigate World Wide Import-Export, Inc., to see if anything more could be learned there.

The Inspector General told his New York counterpart that he would make a full report to him when the interrogation of the captured smugglers was completed. In addition, each of the stolen artifacts would be inspected, its original location identified, and the people who had access to that article would be questioned.

Also, the conditions of the disappearance of each artifact would be determined. It was agreed, by both conversant inspectors, that all this would take some time. The Inspector General, however, informed New York that he would be on the phone again as soon as anything which might be of interest to them, was reported. It was six o'clock before Archy and John left Police Headquarters.

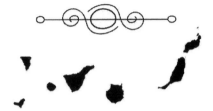

Marilyn Joyce Lafferty Sietsema

CHAPTER XV: Some Answers

The rest of the week was uneventful for John. He worked long hours at the plant with Antonio and Guillermo. Sometimes he accompanied them home after work for dinner with their families. Nothing was heard from Maria. Her clothes remained at Antonio's house. Nancy felt sure something had happened to Maria and was most concerned. She couldn't believe that any girl would leave her clothes, makeup, and personal things of her own volition.

The Inspector General had sent his men to look into Maria's situation at the University. They were informed that she was not registered there and had never lived in the dormitory. A careful search of the records revealed that a young lady from the United States had checked into a dormitory before the school year had started, back in September. She had disappeared a few days later and nothing had been heard from her since. When the school became concerned, they reported her disappearance to the local police. The police did have a record of this in their files but had learned nothing. There was little violent crime on the Islands, so when no body was found, and no one was discovered in the local hospitals, nothing further was done concerning the report. The school had sent a letter to her home address, which came back marked, "No such address - not deliverable."

The police had talked to the dormitory matron who had taken care of the girl on her arrival. She remembered the young man who had accompanied her. She had assumed he was a relative, or a friend of her family. She said she had not been concerned at the time about the girl not being on her registration list. The bursar was sometimes slow in delivering a complete list of names of students who had been accepted and would require accommodations. She told the police that there was no shortage of dormitory rooms and that, frequently, extra students arrived unannounced, even after classes had begun. The police, as a matter of routine, had sent a report to the police in New York, where the girl had purportedly lived. They too checked out the address and found it nonexistent.

Later, several pictures of missing girls of Maria's description, gleaned from the missing persons file, were sent to the matron in an attempt to solve the mystery. None of these attempts proved successful, as the matron did not see a resemblance between any of the pictures and the girl she had checked in. The only thing known for sure was that she had remained in the dormitory less than a week and then left without informing anyone. She took all her belongings with her. The only other girls who had arrived early, before the beginning of classes, had not become particularly friendly with her. They reported that she had been congenial but never talked about herself or her past. No one had gotten to know her very well. She had mentioned that she came from New York and lived there with an aunt. One student remembered that it had come out, in the course of a conversation at the dinner table, that her parents had died when she was young.

The information the students were able to recall could fit with that which Maria had given John. She had told him many things that were not true, also. She had certainly not been living at the dormitory or attending school, as she claimed, when she had become his translator.

There was no absolute assurance that the girl at the dormitory, who had given her name as Jeanne Babcock, was the same person as Maria Albareda. The matron's description of her, and of the man who brought her to the dorm, certainly correlated well with Maria and Wayne, however.

This new information about Maria raised several questions. What was her real name? Where had she been living when she reported for work as a translator at the plant? Where was she now? All evidence pointed to her as a co-conspirator with whoever was responsible for organization of the efforts to defraud the Islands of their valuable relics.

When John questioned Antonio about the application Maria had filled out when she applied for the job of translator, Antonio requested her file from his secretary. She returned later to report that the file was missing. She could not tell John and Antonio when she had last seen the file. She remembered that she had put it in the proper employment file, the same day Maria had reported to work. She had not had an occasion to look at it since - until now. Her time record was in the same file, but Maria had not worked long enough for a pay period to have been completed. If she had worked until the end of the current week, Antonio's secretary would have made out a check for her and recorded this, and the hours she had worked, on her time record. Another dead end! Maria was covering her tracks well, John thought. It was becoming more and more evident that Maria was involved with the criminals.

During the remainder of the week, the police were able to discover a few more connections. The authorities reasoned that the relics had been crated for overseas shipment. The crates were of the type required by most shipping lines when fragile merchandise was shipped overseas. However, none of the captured smugglers could, or would, say where the crates were taken after they were put aboard La Senora. According to their story, they helped remove the items from their original owners, brought them to the cave, and crated them. About once a month, they were called upon to load the crates into the dinghies, and escort them to La Senora. This was done with great caution, usually on a night when the moon was not too bright. The men involved had asked no questions. They had been paid in cash after each loading, by the captain.

The owner of the restaurant where John was held captive was also questioned. He admitted that he was the one who received the orders as to what was to be stolen from the local churches and homes. All his contacts were by phone. He received his orders from a man who kept his voice well muffled. It had been necessary, many times, to have orders repeated. The caller always had him repeat his instructions to make sure he had understood them correctly.

When asked how this all started, he explained that he had received a phone call one evening telling him of a hand carved wooden cross, located in a small niche, in the entrance of the cathedral in Candelaria. He was told that if he could obtain this article, he would be well paid for it. The payment mentioned was more than the restaurant owner could hope to make in a week. He was greatly in debt and saw an opportunity to get out from under it. He reasoned that it was a small, insignificant item, among all the church treasures. He agreed to the arrangement. He was to steal the object when he had the opportunity and keep it hidden until he received another call. The restauranteur did as he was told. About a week later, the caller informed him that the item would be picked up on a particular night. This occurred on schedule, and he was paid in cash, according to arrangements. An announcement was made at church about the missing cross. It was thought that a tourist had been responsible.

Several weeks later, another request was made. The man complied. Again, a tourist was deemed the culprit. Precautions were taken to assure that no further objects would be removed. Tourists were no longer allowed free access to the cathedral. Groups were organized and taken on tours for which fees were charged - to pay for the services of the tour guides. Usually, the guides were recruited from among university students.

The next time the caller made contact, it was suggested that articles be taken from the storerooms, where missing things would not be so easily discerned. For this task, the restaurant owner sought out one of his friends who was a custodian of the church. He was charged with keeping the doors to the storerooms locked after volunteers completed their weekly dusting and polishing tasks. Most of the things stolen from these chambers were never reported because there were so many; they were stored in such complete confusion, never put back in the same location twice, and not cataloged. Even the priests were not aware of all the church's treasures. For hundreds of years, valuable articles that belonged to the church were held sacred. No one in the villages would have dreamed of taking anything - even those who made a business of robbing others.

After several months, the caller recommended articles from other churches and private homes as suitable objects for pilfer. To this end, the restaurant owner recruited men from other towns. Thus, the gang gradually grew in size until it reached its current number.

The police had investigated the crimes but could obtain no real leads. The caller had instructed all the men to wear gloves and to be diligent about throwing away whatever shoes or boots they wore during their sorties so the police would not be able to trace their footprints. Some of the men had even purchased inexpensive, extra-large shoes, and stuffed the toes with paper. They felt that this would prevent the police from determining their actual shoe sizes. Whenever possible, they brushed away any unavoidable prints. They usually didn't work on wet nights. Mostly, there were so many footprints in the churches they looted, that leaving telltale prints was not a problem.

After six months of fairly active pilfering, the group had been informed of the cave site and earned extra money crating the objects that had been stolen by themselves and, apparently, others. Sometimes lumber for the crates was already at the cave when they arrived. Other times it was delivered to the restaurant by truck. The men had no idea where the other objects they crated came from. They assumed that the man who contacted them also contacted others in Tenerife.

When asked about Maria, all the men said they had never seen or heard of her before they saw her in the restaurant. The restaurant owner said that when John and Maria came in that Sunday afternoon, he thought they were tourists. The restaurant owner had been surprised and somewhat frightened when Maria cornered him in the kitchen and told him that John had discovered that they were involved in the thefts. She told him that John must be taken prisoner unless they all wanted to be exposed. The owner was reluctant, but Maria convinced him that she spoke for the "boss" and that it was necessary. The other men supported the restaurant owner's story and added that there was no way they could have confirmed the orders, as they had no phone number they could call.

So far, the criminals had confessed to the thefts, but had denied any connection with the murder. However, John's photographic efforts were about to pay off, and in a big way. When the processed film and prints arrived later in the week, the Santa Cruz police went to work and found the proof they needed. Two of the seventeen footprints John had photographed in the cave, where Wayne's body was discovered, could be identified. The jailed smugglers, thus identified, vigorously denied any knowledge of that crime. This was to be expected. It was one thing to be indicted for theft and smuggling, but quite another to be accused of murder.

Archy remarked afterwards that another reason they may have denied, so adamantly, that their footprints could not have been in the cave, might have been because they were so sure their footprints had been eradicated after Wayne's body had been taken to Tacoronte. At this point, John recalled the lights he had seen at the cave site, when he turned to look back, just before he reached the village of Tequeste. They must have belonged to whoever had been assigned the task of getting rid of the prints. It was probably someone from Tacoronte.

The tire tracks and footprints at the scenic observation point, across from the cave, had not been identified as belonging to any of the smugglers who had been taken into custody. It was quite possible, of course, that these prints belonged to people who were not involved. All the other footprints in the cave could be linked to John, the policeman, Archy, or the men from the village who had helped. The police had made a careful tally.

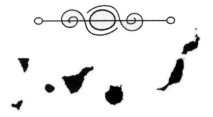

CHAPTER XVI: The Artist Revisited

As the week wore on, John got to thinking more about the artist, Sr. Rendez, in Candelaria. In the excitement of the past weekend adventure, he had not thought to mention him either to Archy or to the police. His visit to Sr. Rendez' studio with Maria had led to John's conjecturing that Rendez might be assisting the thieves to steal valuable paintings. What the priest had said about reproductions being substituted for original paintings kept coming to the foreground in John's thinking. The priest had believed that this was an attempt to keep officials of the church from discovering the thefts until the originals were safely out of the country and virtually unrecoverable.

John also recalled that the priest had said that Rendez never attended mass but did spend a great deal of time looking at the paintings in the chapel. Rendez could, of course, have been merely interested in the paintings from an artist's standpoint. John thought of several more questions he would like to ask the priest. He would like to know if Rendez spent as much time looking at the reproductions as he did at the originals. He would also like to know if Rendez had been responsible for the discovery of any of the fakes. John would have thought it likely that with his artistic talent, he would have been able to spot irregularities rather easily.

As he thought more about the matter, it came to his mind that Rendez had acted somewhat reticent when John had first enquired about Wayne. He thought he had seemed relieved when Maria revealed that they were friends of Wayne's. John decided to drive down to Candelaria again and talk to the priest. It was Saturday morning before he could find time to do this.

When he arrived at the Basilica de Candelaria, he located the priest. He was glad the priest had a reasonable command of English because he had not thought to bring a translator. The priest was glad to see John and welcomed him with open arms. He told him how grateful he and the entire congregation were that he had found the long-lost statue of the Virgin of Candelaria.

"The return of this most precious lady makes up in a way for the many things we have so recently lost." He told John that the statue was now in the process of being restored to a more respectable condition. The priest was agreeable to answering John's questions, although he didn't understand his reason for asking them. The priest disclosed that Sr. Rendez only liked to look at original paintings. In fact, he had mentioned to the priest after the reproductions were discovered that there was no point in his looking at them. He said he wanted to learn nothing about the techniques of a painter who copied other artists' works.

The priest was able to tell John that Sr. Rendez had not been the one to discover the imposter paintings. One of the older priests, Father Gregorino, had been the one to discover them. It seems that Father Gregorino had always been a great admirer of early religious art. Since his assignment to the Basilica at Candelaria, twenty-five years before, he had regularly taken great pleasure in looking at each of the precious paintings in the chapel at least once each month. He had always taken the priest with him on these tours and discussed the details of each picture.

The priest admitted that he did not have an eye for art but enjoyed discussing the paintings with Father Gregorino. Sometimes the father would point out miniscule cracks or chips that had appeared in the paintings and would admonish the priest to place bowls of water about the chapel for a short while to raise the humidity. Usually this was not necessary for very long, as the humidity in the Islands was just about perfect for the preservation of oil paintings. It was only occasionally, during the summer months, that the air became drier.

One day toward the end of October, Father Gregorino stopped before an especially remarkable portrait of the Virgin and child and turned to the priest and demanded, "Why have you replaced the original painting with this reproduction?"

The priest, of course, knew nothing about any of the art being replaced by reproductions. Father Gregorino was so adamant about the switch, that the priest arranged to have an expert from the Prado Museum in Madrid inspect the painting. Father Gregorino was correct. The painting of the Virgin and child was not the original. Between Sr. Gonzales from the Prado and Father Gregorino, they found that six pieces of art were fakes. According to the priest, this was a terrible scandal, and the congregation was most upset.

The police were called in and a thorough investigation was made. The problem was, there was no one to suspect. People living in Candelaria all know one another very well. Someone would know if one of their friends had a painting hanging in their house which might have been stolen. Many people were questioned, but no one could report having seen any stranger acting suspiciously around the church. Of course, there are many tourists who visit the church every year. For the most part, however, they just come to the Cathedral, view the interior, leave and are not seen again. No one was able to report any one person or persons remaining in the area longer than usual or returning many times.

"I have tried, since then, to keep an eye on the chapel at all times. When I am away, I always arrange for someone else to keep a watchful eye on our beautiful cathedral. It is a real pity," lamented the priest. "For so many years we have never had to worry about such things. Now it seems as if we must, of necessity, suspect everyone."

"John asked, "What was Sr. Rendez' reaction when he learned of the forgeries?"

"Well, I don't know precisely when he learned about them, but I do recall that he commented to me that the reproductions were unusually good."

"Do you have any reason to suspect that Sr. Rendez may have had a part in this skullduggery?"

"Oh, dear me, no. I would be reluctant to implicate anyone in such a diabolical escapade. He is not even a member of our congregation."

John thanked the priest for his help and gave him one of his business cards on which he had written Antonio's phone number. He requested that he call him if he thought of anything else that might be helpful in the investigation. He also told him that his was an unofficial investigation and that he planned to pass on the information the priest had given him to Inspector

General de Lugo when he contacted him later in the day. The priest told John that he hoped Sr. Rendez had had nothing to do with the disappearance of the artwork. He did not like to think that anyone in Candelaria would be involved in such an unthinking act. "Someone from another village perhaps, but not from our town."

John left the Basilica and returned to his car. He drove around to the side of the Basilica that overlooked the ocean. It was a spectacular location. He took a few moments to photograph the façade of the building and then turned his attention to the ocean. The sea was calm against a bright blue sky with only a few fluffy clouds to lend character to the scene. Reluctantly, John left the scenery behind, climbed into the car and drove up to the residential section where Sr. Rendez had his studio. Feeling unsure about parking his car on the steep grade again, he parked the car at the bottom of the hill and walked up the long narrow street. When he reached the halfway point, he looked back to admire another view of the Basilica and the ocean below. The street was almost deserted. There were several elderly widows dressed in black, scarves over their heads, sitting in the doorways he passed. Most of them, heads bent, worked diligently on some sort of needlework. In some cases, John guessed, the objects they were making would be sold for money to augment their meager incomes. He nodded and they returned his greeting.

As he neared the artist's studio one older lady smiled and said, "Good Afternoon."

"You speak English?" he responded.

"Yes, I was born and raised in England. You don't sound like an Englishman."

"No, I'm an American," replied John. "Do you know Sr. Rendez?"

"Yes, quite well. He was married to my daughter."

"Was married?" questioned John.

"Yes, she died when their last baby was born. It was such a shock for Francis. It has been so sad for him, being alone all these years."

"How long ago did she die?"

"Oh, it has been about 11 years. He is a good man. He works very hard painting so he can support us - myself and his nine children. Of course, all the children are away at school or on their own now, except for Ramondo. He stays with me. I take care of him in my house and cook for both my youngest grandson and his father."

"Is Sr. Rendez in now?"

"No, I don't think so, but you may look if you like. The door is usually unlocked. Sometimes he is gone for several weeks when he travels to the other end of Tenerife to paint the scenery there. I have not seen his old truck parked behind the studio since last Monday. He usually tells me when he is going on a trip, but he must have forgotten this time. I am almost sure he is still not back in the studio."

"That's too bad," sighed John. "I was here last Sunday afternoon and would like to take another look at some of his paintings."

"Since you are a prospective customer, go ahead into the studio and look as long as you wish. Many people do this. We are not formal around here. His paintings are beautiful. I'm sure you will find something you like. If you do, you can set it aside with me and come back and buy it when he returns. I am sorry that I do not know the prices of the pictures." At this point, a very handsome young boy of eleven or twelve arrived home. His grandmother said goodbye to John and, in the manner of a doting grandmother, hurried inside the house with the boy.

John took advantage of Sr. Rendez' mother-in-law's offer and went on up to the studio. He tried the door handle and, as she had predicted, the door was unlocked. The inside was about like it had been when John had last visited the studio. There did not seem to be nearly as many paintings, however. John estimated that at least half of the artwork was gone. He made a mental note to stop by the grandmother's house on the way back and ask if he was having a showing of the missing paintings or if they had been sold. He didn't think so many would have been sold in the past week.

As he looked around, he noticed that there were few religious paintings left. Most of the pictures he could see were still-life paintings or landscapes. One especially caught his eye. It was a view of the ocean as seen from the Basilica. It could have been painted at the very same spot where John had stood and taken a picture with his camera a short while before. He was no art critic, but the paintings looked rather well executed to John. In fact, he wanted to purchase it when the artist returned if it had not already been spoken for. Looking about him, he could see three doors at the end of the studio away from the street. He opened each in turn.

One led to a small room with a bed in it. John thought this must be where Sr. Rendez slept. A few items of clothing were scattered about, and the bed was unmade. This room had two other doors, one which led to a small bathroom. This also was in some disarray. The other door exposed a closet when opened. This contained several very old frames without pictures and clothing as would be expected. The frames were what caught John's attention. They resembled, very closely, the ones he had seen in the cathedral. They were large and very ornate. He saw nothing else of interest in the closet, so returned to the studio to investigate the other two doors.

The second door he tried disclosed a circular metal staircase. John climbed the stairs and reached a storage room at the top. This attic-like room had inside shutters which were closed. The room seemed very dark after the brightness of the studio below. He felt along the walls for a light switch but could find none. He regretted that he had left his flashlight behind. After bumping into boxes of one kind or another, he finally reached the windows and pulled open the shutters. Now that the room was sufficiently bright, John could see several crates. These were of a size and shape such as one might expect to find holding paintings. This was not surprising. Sr. Rendez probably took the responsibility for crating and shipping many of the paintings he sold to foreign tourists. These crates did look very much like some of the ones he had seen in the cave. But then he thought, "A crate is a crate is a crate."

What did disturb him were two very old looking oil paintings standing against the wall ready to be crated. They had tiny cracks and chips and were dark with age and grime. It seemed unlikely to John that these could have been painted by Sr. Rendez. It was possible that the artist was going to restore the

174

paintings for a client. The priest had very definitely not mentioned Sr. Rendez being called upon to restore any of the paintings belonging to the cathedral.

Perhaps he should consider asking the priest about this before he returned to Santa Cruz. Nothing else in the room seemed to have any significance. Closing the shutters and leaving everything as he had found it, he retraced his steps down to the studio and tried the third door.

Feeling around for a light switch, he found one and turned it on. There appeared to be a dangerously decrepit flight of stairs leading down to a cellar lighted by only one bulb. He worked his way carefully down the rickety, unsafe ghost of a staircase until he reached the hard packed dirt floor at the bottom. He had little taste for the exploration, as it reminded him of his internment in the restaurant's musty wine cellar. He sorely wished he had informed someone reliable of his whereabouts. As his eyes became accustomed to the dim light, he saw that all was not right. A dark form hung by a rope from the rafters. Closer inspection brought John to the realization that it was Sr. Rendez. He was dead.

It looked, at first glance, as if Sr. Rendez must have committed suicide. A chair appeared to have been toppled to its side just underneath him. His feet almost touched the floor, and the rope was stretched tautly around his neck. The artist's head slumped grotesquely forward and to one side. His cheeks were puffed and swollen. Blood had trickled from his nose, dribbled past his lips, and dried before quite reaching his chin. John was grateful that his eyes were closed. If they had been open, it would have added even more horror to that which he was already experiencing. Not having a flashlight, he could not examine the body particularly well. Only dim light was afforded by the bare bulb overhead. What did catch John's attention were slight red chafe marks on both wrists. The victim's arms hung limply at his sides.

Apprehensively, he hurried quickly back up the stairs, turned off the light switch, and closed the cellar door. With alacrity he left the studio and hastened down the hill to where the car was parked. He wondered if he should first inform the Inspector General or the priest. The nearest phone was probably in the cathedral. He decided to go there. Fortunately, the priest was still in the chapel. John explained what he had found at Sr. Rendez' studio. The priest was most sympathetic and assured John that he would tell the grandmother and Sr. Rendez' son about the tragic event.

John used the phone in the priest's office to call Inspector General de Lugo. The Inspector General listened as John gave him all the details of his accidental discovery of the artist's body.

He rationalized that he had been interested in looking at some paintings with the possibility of purchasing one. He also admitted that he had wanted to talk again with the artist in hopes of learning more about the art reproductions hanging in the chapel. He disclosed that he had not stayed long enough in the cellar to examine the body very carefully. He mentioned that it was obvious that the artist's death was meant to look like suicide, but he wondered if that would prove to be the case. He told him about the chafe marks he had noticed on the victim's wrists. He also communicated to the Inspector General concerning the old-looking paintings and the shipping crates in the attic and the antique frames in the bedroom closet.

The Inspector General informed John that he would take care of everything. He insisted that John return to his hotel at once. "It is possible," suggested de Lugo, "that you may be in extreme danger if certain people are aware that you are still investigating Wayne's murder. It is evident to me that not all of the culprits in this case are behind bars. Leave the rest of this case to us. Let me talk to the priest. I want the rest of the population to think that the body was discovered entirely accidentally. Perhaps we can arrange it so no one will know that you were involved."

He added with some emphasis, "Get back in your car and leave at once!"

John agreed and left after handing the phone to the priest.

It was noon when he arrived back at the hotel. Now that he was thoroughly involved in the Canary Island Caper, as he had begun to think of it, he realized that the mystery must be solved before more people were killed.

He didn't know whether his early interest in the artist, when he had visited the studio with Maria, had ultimately led to his death or not. He thought it had led to his own internment in the wine cellar.

If it hadn't been for Archy, John felt certain he would have met with a fate similar to that of Sr. Rendez. He was sure the smugglers would not have returned him unharmed to his hotel after he had witnessed their operation on the beach.

After eating a light lunch, he returned to his room. The Inspector General had warned him to remain in his room, with his door locked securely, until the Inspector General phoned him. This was going to be difficult for him as John was eager to inform the Inspector General of his earlier visit with Maria to the Rendez studio. This was something he had not thought to mention in his earlier phone call.

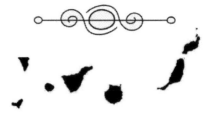

CHAPTER XVII: Death Rediscovered

Sunday, when John had not heard from the Inspector General, he made the decision to relax and enjoy taking photographs. He also couldn't resist indulging in a bit more sleuthing. It bothered him that the question of where the crates were taken, after being put aboard La Senora, had not been answered.

The Inspector General had told John that his men had questioned other boat owners, including those who had boats in slips near La Senora. Unfortunately, these owners had not noticed any crates being unloaded at any time from the captain's boat. The police had talked to the proprietors of stalls along the quay, the small tavern owners located on the street just above the quay, the bait shop personnel, and the refreshment hawkers. Considering the large number of boxes that had been in the cave when he first discovered it, John thought it reasonable to assume that at some time, someone would have noticed at least one crate or box being unloaded from or transported to La Senora. The bait shops were open very early in the morning and the refreshment stands and taverns remained open until late at night.

John decided that his first trip Sunday morning would be to Puerto de la Cruz. It was an excellent place for scenic photos, with its fine black sand beaches and picturesque boardwalk. Also, he thought he might gain some further insights into the possible disposition of the artifacts which had been taken aboard the boat.

He spent several hours photographing the sights in Puerto de la Cruz. He was fascinated by another photographer who earned his living taking pictures of people holding a tame lion cub. John approached him, "Where did your lion cub come from?"

The young man spoke excellent English and replied, "From Africa. His mama was shot by a hunter who did not realize she had a cub. He said I could have him, but he would be a lot of work. He was right. This little fellow is hungry all the time."

"What do you feed him?" John asked as he patted the wiggling cub gingerly on its head.

"He gets goat's milk and ground meat. The veterinarian also gave me some kind of vitamin and mineral pill which he loves to chew on."

"What are you going to do with him when he gets too big to carry around?"

"The zoo in Madrid has already agreed to take him. He has such a sweet disposition; he should be a joy to the caretakers there."

"Are you here every day taking pictures?"

"I am somewhere along the boardwalk every day. I try to stay where the crowds are."

"Have you ever taken pictures back by the fishing docks?"

"If you mean where the fishing boats are moored, yes. I don't spend a lot of time there as there are not so many customers. I am there sometimes - usually in the early part of the morning."

"Have you ever observed any large crates being unloaded from a boat called La Senora?"

"Oh, I never pay much attention to the names of the boats. Is it a large boat or a small one?"

"It is a medium sized fishing boat. There are probably a few that are slightly larger."

"I have only seen boxes of fish being unloaded from any of the boats. The boxes are all about the same size and usually have water dripping from them. I tell you, that is one job I wouldn't like to have. I don't like the smell of fish. Why are you interested?"

"I am interested in the types of commercial products coming into Puerto de la Cruz," John equivocated."

"Well, I guess I haven't been much help."

"I have enjoyed talking with you very much. Good luck with your little friend."

As noon approached, more and more people ambled along the board walk, with its sandy black beach on one side and the vendor's stalls on the other. One stand had dozens of brightly colored parrots for sale. Another sold paper cups filled with fruit flavored ices in brilliant crayon colors. A gypsy organ grinder featured a nattily dressed monkey who turned summersaults and exhibited his toothy grin for the payment of a few coins into his small cup.

Many different languages could be heard from the variety of visitors. John heard a vacationing Dutch family speaking one of the harsh sounding dialects of that country. A sexy nursemaid, wearing a black dress trimmed with a crisp white lace collar and cuffs, held a charming Italian toddler by each hand. Slightly older children pranced happily with colorful balloons tied to their wrists. Plump, elderly ladies waddled along in groups, while their trim husbands trailed behind. An elegant dowager made her way carefully with an ornately clipped dog, bedecked in an expensive jeweled collar, tugging impatiently at his leash.

A dignified English gentlemen contrasted sharply with the colorfully dressed, blustering German tourists. One young, shy Greek couple appeared to be on their honeymoon. John photographed much of this. The children were especially appealing. He took many pictures of some very young and not so young bathing beauties sunning themselves in their bikinis on the dark sand. John attempted several other conversations, but many of the people did not speak English. Those that did had seen nothing that would be of any help to him.

John returned to his car about noon and spent the next hour driving around Puerto de la Cruz. He was looking for warehouse space where the treasure boxes might have been sequestered. He located nothing that seemed suitable. Of course, the basement of any shop along the main street might have been used, but surely someone would have noticed the crates being unloaded along the quay.

Having satisfied himself that he had taken his quota of interesting photos and that there was little left to investigate in Puerto de la Cruz, John drove back to Santa Cruz. Again, along the Autopista he found himself in a long line of banana trucks. He thought them fascinating and, on the spur of the moment, decided to follow them to wherever they were going. They led him into Santa Cruz and down to the main dock area where numerous large ocean liners and freight steamers from the continent were docked.

The banana trucks drove down a long ramp to the cement quay below. John parked on the street above the quay, easing the front of his VW almost against the iron railing that kept parked cars from inadvertently joining the activities below. He got out of his car, looked over the railing, and slinging his camera bag over his shoulder, made his way down the ramp on foot.

Huge cranes were lifting large crates aboard the ships. The bananas were being lifted in nets by large winches. It was a busy and bustling scene. John used his camera to record the many activities and operations on the dock. Several longshoremen spotted him taking pictures. They laughingly grouped themselves into a humorous charade and gestured for John to take their picture. One rough fellow, his straggly hair topped by a dirty and ragged knitted cap, spoke some English. He called for John to take a picture of him. "I'm a handsome fellow, eh? All the girls are crazy about me!" John complied with the request, joining in with the laughter. When the men returned to work, John wandered among the boxes stacked along the dock.

Some crates contained fresh vegetables; tomatoes, celery, lettuce, and onions, destined for the markets of Europe. Huge baskets of fresh flowers were probably going to the florist shops of Belgium or Germany. The exotic Bird of Paradise flowers were carefully handled and would soon be found in elegant arrangements delivered, possibly, to Paris addresses. The sights, sounds, and smells intrigued John. The smells, emitting from the boxes piled high on the quay, reminded him of a farmers' market in the United States.

Not only were goods being loaded, but cargo was also being unloaded for use in the Canary Islands. John saw a crate of butter from Belgium dropped from its hook. The crate smashed as it hit the cement. John guessed that this particular lot of butter would end up in cakes or on vegetables, rather than on the table. Sides of beef and lamb were removed from the refrigerated hold of yet another ship and wheeled on a rack to a waiting refrigerated truck.

The sight of all this food made John realize that he had not eaten lunch. It was about three o'clock when he made his way back up the ramp. He had just settled himself into his car when he noticed a sleek, black sedan drive past the rear of his parked VW. It was sufficiently attention-getting to draw his scrutiny, as well as that of others. He stepped out of his car and followed the vehicle with his eyes as it slowly traversed the ramp. The sedan was chauffeur driven and he could just see the leg portions of a man and woman who were seated in the back. The limousine drove slowly along the quay, eliciting whistles from the longshoremen John had photographed.

When the car stopped, an elderly gentleman dressed in a neat gray suit, a Panama hat shading his face, stepped from the sedan. The door on the other side was opened by the chauffeur to permit a trim young lady, with flowing brown hair, dressed in a crisp white linen suit, to emerge. John recognized the young lady at once - it was Maria. He was certain he had not seen the man before. John quickly got out his camera and, peering through his telephoto lens, was able to confirm that the girl was, indeed, Maria. She was not dressed in the casual student attire he was used to seeing her in, but rather, appeared to be a sophisticated lady of high fashion.

He quickly snapped a few pictures, both of the gentleman as he turned to glance around the quay, and of Maria, when she glanced back at the baskets of flowers he had photographed earlier. John made sure he had several good shots of the limousine, including its license plate. The couple went up the passenger ramp of one of the large ocean liners. It appeared to be of Spanish register. One could see that it was loading cargo as well. Earlier, he had observed tourists leaving the same ship and boarding a tour bus which had probably taken them on a shopping trip and perhaps a more extended tour of Tenerife. Since the bus had left such a short time ago, John surmised that the boat would not be leaving Santa Cruz in the near future. His best guess was that it would leave port either late at night or sometime the following day.

After Maria and the gentleman boarded the ship, the chauffeur followed with luggage which he handed to a cabin attendant before returning to the limousine. He did not drive off but sat as if waiting for someone to return. Traffic on the quay divided and flowed around the limousine. Because the chauffeur had not bothered to pull the car over to the side and had not taken off his jacket and started to buff the car, John guessed that he expected to be driving away in a short while. John continued to watch, and soon the gentleman left the ship and got back into the limousine. The driver carefully turned the car around, returned up the ramp, and drove off.

John's first impulse was to enter the ship and try and locate Maria. Instead, he made a decision he was to regret later. He drove directly to police headquarters and asked to see Inspector General de Lugo. John did not have to wait but was shown into his office immediately. "You have thought of something more to tell me?" queried the Inspector General.

John described what he had seen.

"Are you sure it was the girl Maria?" asked de Lugo.

"Absolutely!" replied John. "I took pictures of Maria, the gentleman, and the car."

"Perhaps you would be so kind as to leave the film with us," said the Inspector General with a twinkle in his eyes. "We really do have a laboratory that is quite capable of processing just about any type of film."

"Yes, of course," replied John. He removed the partly completed roll of film from his camera. As he handed it to the Inspector General, he asked if the negatives and prints not pertaining to the case could be saved for him.

The Inspector General responded, "Yes, certainly!" "I suggest," he continued, "that you accompany us to the ship and that we try to find out just what part Maria has played in this case."

John remembered the license number of the limousine and the name of the ship. The Inspector General had one of his aides look these up. A few minutes later, he returned to inform them that the limousine and the ship belonged to Senor Manuel Phillip Martinez. He also confirmed that the ship was not scheduled to leave port until late in the evening.

"Senor Martinez," said the Inspector General, "is a very wealthy man and a pillar of the community. He is the owner of a number of luxury liners and cargo ships that carry goods and passengers between many cities on the European Continent and the Canary Islands. Are you absolutely sure this young girl who was with him was Maria?"

"As sure as I can be," countered John.

"All right, we will board the ship, try and find her, and question her. If you can identify her, we will bring her in for questioning. Archy said he saw her too, when he found you bound and gagged in the restaurant at Candelaria. He should be able to give us a second positive identification. With a positive identification from the two of you, and perhaps from one or two of the smugglers we are holding, we may be able to hold her for a more intensive interrogation. We could have a problem, however, with Senor Martinez. He has a reputation for being fond of young women and may defend her rights if she decides to appeal to him."

John accompanied the Inspector General and four policemen. They took two cars and leisurely made their way through the streets of Santa Cruz, down to the quay. During the drive, John questioned the Inspector General, "Can you tell me what you've learned about Sr. Rendez?"

"Yes, he was murdered. There is no doubt about that. A rather good attempt was made to make it look like suicide. The chair had been placed in the exact spot it would have been expected to be in, had the artist actually committed suicide. There were, however, several discrepancies. For one thing, you mentioned that the cellar was dark until you turned on the light. It is improbable that Rendez would have been able to perform an act of suicide in the absolute complete darkness of that basement. Besides, there would have been no reason for him to do so. He would have been more likely to leave the light on."

"I had thought about that too."

"In addition," continued de Lugo, "we confirmed your observation of chafe marks on his wrists. The coroner said his hands must have been tied for quite a while. Also, forensic laboratory tests showed that the artist was so heavily drugged that he would not have had the necessary coordination to perpetrate the suicide."

"Do you have any idea who may have murdered Sr. Rendez?"

"No, not at this time. We did talk to his mother-in-law. She admitted that her son had been more free with money in the past year than previously. She is convinced, however, that it was because he had more customers."

"Did you show her a picture of Wayne?"

"Yes, and she did recognize him. It seems that Mr. Morrison came to the studio, regularly, about once a month and selected paintings from the artist's finished stock. Rendez crated the pictures for him, and they were picked up by a man driving an old truck."

"Do you think she would recognize the driver of the truck and the truck itself, if she saw them again?"?

"We had her view photographs of all of the men we had taken into custody. She did not think any of them were the driver of the truck."

"Did you question the boy?"

"Yes, he told us that when the truck arrived to pick up the crated paintings, it frequently already had boxes of different sizes and shapes in it. He had seen the driver and the truck several times, so we showed him the same photographs we had shown his grandmother. He did not recognize the driver among them either. He did tell us something else that was quite interesting though. He remembered looking out his bedroom window one night after he had been to the bathroom. He saw a man carry a picture up the hill and take it into his father's studio. The next day he stopped at the studio on his way to school to ask his father for money for a book. He saw what was probably the same picture leaning against the wall of his father's bedroom. It had an ornate frame and looked very old. He said the picture itself looked just like one he had watched his father paint earlier. I asked the boy if his father painted pictures so that they looked old, very often. He said that he sometimes did, as the tourists liked them that way."

"You are convinced then that Sr. Rendez was involved in making the reproductions that were substituted for the originals?"

"Yes, I think that is pretty certain. I am not sure why he was killed. After talking with the priest, I find it possible to believe that Sr. Rendez did not approve of what he himself was doing. He may even have been forced into doing it. As to why he was killed, that is difficult to say. It may have been because the girl, Maria, was convinced he might be questioned if you told us about your visit with her to his studio. She might have predicted that you would associate your visit to the artist's studio and your subsequent kidnapping. Someone might have been afraid that Sr. Rendez would break down and tell what he knew under questioning."

"I wish I had thought to tell you or Archy sooner about my earlier visit to the studio. I guess there were just too many other events to discuss. I completely forgot about it."

"Well, we don't know for sure that your earlier visit there had anything to do with it. Sr. Rendez may not have liked what he was doing and decided to quit of his own accord. This might have been what determined his death. We are dealing with an unscrupulous group."

"There is something else I need to mention. Do you remember that I told you I thought I had seen Wayne at the Mencey the first night I was there? Did you ever check that out?"

"Yes, one of my men went over the occupant files of the hotel. They found that Mr. Morrison had stayed at the Mencey frequently during the past several years. However, he was not registered there just prior to his death. We also checked other hotels in Santa Cruz and Puerto de la Cruz. He was not registered in any of these hotels either."

"I came away with the same conclusion when I first discussed the matter with the reservations clerk at the front desk. Later however, when I looked through the card file again, this time with a more patient clerk, he discovered something interesting. A Mr. William Morton had checked into the hotel the same day as I had - the day I thought I saw Wayne. He had made reservations through Sunday. When Sunday evening came, he did not check out. Nor did he check out during the following week or contact the reservations desk. Furthermore, the maid confirmed that Mr. Morton had not occupied his room since Saturday when he had checked in. I was able to convince the clerk that we ought to take a look in his room. We did so, and I recognized the suit Wayne had worn on the plane hanging in the closet. I also recognized his luggage. We did not open the bags, but the clerk said they would likely store the luggage and other items if they did not hear from Mr. Morton by the following Monday. You might possibly learn something more about Wayne by examining his luggage and other personal items."

"Thank you for this information. I shall have one of my men follow up on this right away. You seem to have become quite involved in this case. Do you have any more information we should know about?"

John assured the Inspector General that he did not. By this time, they had arrived at the quay. The squad cars parked on the lower level, opposite the ramp leading into the liner.

John and the others stepped out of the car. John noticed, as he peered inside the entrance to the ship, that this was definitely a luxury liner. Waiters, in spotless white jackets, were carrying trays of drinks, and the odor of gourmet cooking issued forth from the entrance.

The Inspector General talked briefly to a cabin attendant. The officers and John were led into the ship, up a flight of carpeted stairs, and into the office of the captain. The captain was most cooperative. He was interested in complying with whatever the Inspector General wished and in having the local constabulary leave the ship as quickly as possible. He didn't say this in so many words, but it was evident to John. At the request of the Inspector General he let them examine his passenger list. There was no passenger by the name of Maria Alberada on the list, but neither John nor the Inspector General thought there would be. The captain was able to tell them that there were several young women aboard who would answer Maria's description. When questioned about a young girl who had come aboard less than an hour ago, the captain admitted that she was not on the passenger list. It had been a last-minute decision to board her, and they had not had time to add her to the official list. He had not yet been informed of her name. One of his officers had received a call from Senor Martinez earlier in the day requesting space for another passenger, and since they had the room, they granted his request. The captain put in a call to the cabin attendant who was responsible for the area she was lodged in. When he arrived, he revealed that the young lady had given her name as Janice St. John.

The Inspector General requested that the cabin attendant take them to her cabin as they wished to ask her a few questions. The captain, with a worried look on his face, inquired, "There is nothing irregular in taking on a passenger that we had not planned for, is there?"

"No!" growled the Inspector General. "But did this young woman have a passport and other identification?"

The captain turned to the cabin attendant for an answer. He looked blank and retorted, "I thought, Sir, that all of that had been taken care of when I was sent to bring her to her room."

"Take us to her room!" the Inspector General demanded crisply.

The captain obtained a key to the room, led the officers and John up another flight of stairs to the main cabin deck and down a long carpeted hall, past mahogany walls and doors with gleaming brass knobs. When they reached the room., the captain knocked lightly on the door. When no one answered, he remarked, "She may be up on deck or taking a tour of the ship." He turned to the cabin attendant, "Did you see her leave the cabin?"

The cabin attendant replied, "No Sir! I deposited her bags in her closet and, after determining that she had no immediate wishes, I left the room and closed the door behind. I have not seen her since. I ran several errands for other passengers, but she did not require my services. I have no knowledge of where she is."

The captain knocked again, several times - always discreetly - as he didn't wish to draw the attention of other passengers to the police officers. At the Inspector General's request, the captain unlocked the stateroom door. They could see that the bags were properly stored in the entry closet as the cabin attendant had said they were. There was no one in the tiny bathroom opposite the entry closet. Then they saw her. It could not have been determined who, exactly, saw her first. She was draped limply over the bed, on her back, her body distorted in an unnatural fashion. The bed was still made. Her shoes were on her feet, although somewhat askew.

The meticulous white suit was still fresh and crisp, accented now by a medallion of deep red at her throat. Even the most hardened of the group could not help gasping at the unmitigated horror of the scene before them. One of the officers took a closer look at the body sprawled across the bed. He felt the pulse of the victim and then quietly shook his head as he let Maria's wrist drop gently back on the bed. There was no doubt in anyone's mind. The girl was dead.

John identified her as Maria. What a pity that such a young person, so full of the joy of life, had come to such a ruthless end. If he had only sought her out before going to the police, perhaps he could have prevented this. He stated as much to the Inspector General. "You must not deride yourself," remarked the Inspector General. "There is no way you could have foretold that this was going to happen. It was only logical that you contact us before intervening. In fact, if you had attempted to contact her on your own, you, too, might have been killed. She had some control over her destiny, I'm sure. The question for us to answer is, 'What was she involved in, to deserve this treatment?'"

John thought to himself, "What a deplorable situation when criminals can take matters into their own hands and kill anyone who stands in their way."

Inspector General de Lugo ushered the captain, cabin attendant, John, and the officers gently out of Maria's cabin. Then he left the room and closed the door quietly. He ordered one of the officers to stand guard. The captain was to phone police headquarters and relay a message that the coroner and detail men be summoned to the ship immediately. The captain was also ordered to delay the ship's departure for another 24 hours. It had been due to leave port around midnight.

The Inspector General invited John to remain and observe the detailed procedure if he wished. He suggested John would be welcome to take photographs along with the official police photographer. John declined, having no stomach for another look at Maria. He had seen enough to realize that she had been ruthlessly stabbed. It seemed likely that she knew her assassin and was not expecting to be attacked. She did not appear to have put up any resistance. Two of the policemen who had accompanied them from headquarters were already knocking on the doors of the adjoining cabins. There were no answers from most of the cabins. The occupants were probably on the tour bus or lounging on one of the sun decks.

John felt there was nothing further he could do so he rode back to the station with one of the returning police officers. When he reached the station, he thanked the policeman and returned to his own car.

He drove back to the hotel in a depressed state of mind. It was nearing six o'clock as he parked his car along a side street. The dining room was quite empty as six o'clock was much too early for Spanish diners. John was shown to a table at the far side of the dining room. The regular dinners were not ready to be served, but he was able to order a mixed salad and broiled fish. While waiting to be served, he munched on crusty hard rolls liberally spread with Belgian butter.

Ordinarily he would have enjoyed his meal, but his mind was on the puzzle of Maria. He hardly noticed what he ate.

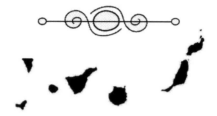

CHAPTER XVIII: A Solution at Last

Two glasses of wine after his meal left John drowsy.

As he ascended to his floor he looked forward to a good night's sleep. He wasn't expected at work on Monday - it was a national holiday and only a skeletal maintenance crew would be on duty. However, he had been invited to have lunch with Antonio and Guillermo and their families. He didn't look forward to breaking the news of Maria's death to Nancy.

Perhaps she would already know. He didn't know if the Inspector General would release Maria's identity to the news media or not. Come to think of it, did they really know who Maria was? The police reports from the U.S. had all been negative with respect to her identity. It was possible that a picture of her would be released to the news, in hopes that someone from the public could identify her. Thinking of her made him sad, and he decided to make an effort to clear these thoughts from his mind. He would call Irene and bring her up to date on the case. She might have additional news too.

He reached the door of his room, fumbled for his keys, finally unlocked the door, and pushed it open. He sensed immediately that something was not right but did not react quickly enough to prevent himself from being grabbed from behind. Someone had been behind the entrance door waiting for him. He struggled, but the meal, wine, and ensuing drowsiness all conspired to make him vulnerable. A snarling Spanish voice gave him orders - to do something or not to do something - he couldn't tell which. When he could feel that his struggling was netting him nothing but bruises and pain, he decided to give up and use his brain instead of his brawn.

When he ceased his struggling, his captor pushed him face down on the bed. John's hands were quickly tied behind his back and his feet were firmly bound together. A pillowcase was removed from one of the pillows on the bed and pulled over his head.

He could detect two voices. These voices seemed well satisfied with themselves. He heard the click of the doorknob as his room door was cautiously opened. More quiet conversation followed. One of his captors entered the bathroom and turned on the faucet in the sink. In a few minutes he was rolled to one side and the pillowcase was pulled part way off. A wet washcloth was stuffed, none too gently, into his mouth.

He could hear the sound and feel the vibrations of a strip of cloth being ripped from the length of the bedsheet he was lying on. This was pulled firmly over his mouth and tied tightly at the back of his neck. It partly covered his nose as well, which made breathing difficult. It was an effective way of keeping him quiet. He could not make a sound, even to protest the strip of sheet covering his nose. The pillowcase was pulled back down over his head.

By remaining still, he could just barely take enough oxygen into his lungs to keep him from passing out. All was quiet, and then a low guttural order was issued. He was lifted and carried from the room. He could still only discern two thugs.

They carried him a great distance down a hall in the opposite direction from the elevators. A door was pushed open by the man carrying his head. He could hear it close with a soft thud when his feet were past it. A few seconds later, his head was lower than his feet. His body was jerked back and forth to the motion of the men descending a flight of stairs.

When they reached the ground floor, according to John's counting of the landings, his body was folded over at the waist and dumped into a container. It smelled like a dirty laundry hamper. The sides were fabric, and he was able to comfortably rest his head against one side. Material, probably used bed linen, was deposited on top of him and the hamper was pushed ahead on its wheels.

John was wheeled through several entries and down a short incline. He felt himself and the container lifted upward and heard the muffled sound of van doors being closed with a slam and then a firm click.

He must have been driven for quite a distance. It was difficult to tell. He did manage to rearrange his body by pushing with his feet. Some of the sheets on top of him slipped down beside him and breathing became a fraction more assured.

A damp, pungent, musty odor, combined with the smell of stale perfume, food, and body odor, confirmed his earlier suspicion that he was enveloped in dirty laundry. He was actually grateful now for the strip of cloth over his nose. It probably was filtering out some of the most displeasing odors.

John must have dozed off several times because he became suddenly aware that the van had stopped. The van doors were opened, the hamper was rolled out, and he was tumbled onto the ground. His body was pulled onto a sheet, and he was carried into a building and down steps to, what he surmised to be, a cellar. The dank smell permeated even his well-covered nostrils.

His captors released him from his sheet by tipping him to the floor. There was a dim light in the cellar which came from overhead. The pillowcase was yanked from his head, and he could, at last, view his captors.

They were rough longshoreman types but with none of the joviality he had observed in those he had photographed on the quay earlier in the day. He felt certain he had never seen these particular fellows before. He motioned, by moving his head, that the tie was covering his nose too tightly and one of the thugs begrudgingly pushed the strip of sheet down a bit.

The two men glanced at him briefly, looked around the cellar, ascended the stairs, and slammed and locked the door at the top. He had expected them to turn off the light and was surprised when they didn't. He glanced around his prison, rolling his body over to get a better view. He spotted the light switch on the wall next to the stairs. Probably there was no switch at the top of the stairs. This explained why they hadn't turned the light off. This wasn't much consolation.

Closer scrutiny revealed that the cellar looked familiar. Slowly he realized this was Archy's wine cellar.

Perhaps he was confused. No, he was certain the table was identical to the one where Wayne's body had been. Even the wine bottles, which had been removed from the table to make room for the body, were still on the floor. He was confident he was not mistaken.

Many thoughts ran through his mind for the next several hours. He finally fell asleep from the effects of the food, wine, and a long, exhausting day.

When he awoke, it took some time for him to orient himself to his surroundings. Realization as to where he was dawned on him slowly. His wrists and ankles hurt unbelievably. The side he was lying on was sore and tender. Numerous aches and pains abounded over his entire body. His nose itched and he could scratch it only by putting it against a table leg and moving his head back and forth. His mouth was dry and felt like it had been open for hours in a desert. The washcloth, stuffed down into his throat, must have absorbed all the saliva from his mouth. His stomach hurt and he was miserable.

In the seemingly eons that followed, he had time to do a lot of thinking. He tried to consider the significance of his being in Archy's wine cellar. Were his captors not running the risk that Archy or his wife would discover and release him? How likely was it that Archy's wife would not have been home when he was carried through her house? He had heard no voices or any other people moving around. He had, in fact, assumed that he was in an unoccupied building. He heard no movements or sounds now from the floor above.

In a lighter vein, he mentally told himself he was getting tired of being held captive in damp caves and cellars. He rationalized that caves and cellars were generally considered to be suitable quarters for the victims of kidnappings. He did think it would have been preferable to have been interned in an above ground barn or in an old house. He managed to maneuver his body about the floor with great difficulty. Hoping to find some means of freeing himself, he resolved to examine every corner of his underground prison.

Suddenly he heard heavy fast-moving footsteps on the floor above. Abruptly, the door at the top of the stairs opened, and John could see Archy descending the stairs.

Help at last! Thank God! When he got a good look at his face, he did not feel so confident. Archy looked sad and disgusted. He untied the gag and called up to his wife to bring down some water. She did so, setting the glass on the table and retreating without glancing at John. John knew something was wrong.

Archy spoke first, "I'm sorry old man, your curiosity has finally gotten you into serious trouble. I'm afraid we have no choice but to eliminate you. You have discovered too many facts and have interfered too much. I wanted to spare you, but that will be impossible now."

A cold rush of fear enveloped John's body. He was speechless and could only stare at Archy in complete disbelief. Finally, his voice returned. In, what he hoped was a calm voice, he returned, "I thought you were working with the government to solve the smuggling mystery."

"They think so too. It was a real stroke of genius having me hired by the Spanish Intelligence Agency to infiltrate the smuggling ring and finger the participants. What the government doesn't know, is that I am also working with the gang."

"No, I don't believe Inspector General de Lugo would suspect you of being involved in criminal activities. He thinks highly of you."

"That's why this has been such a perfect setup. I have immediate access to any information the police receive and know almost every move they are planning to make. A distinct advantage, wouldn't you say?"

"What are you going to do with me?"

"As I said, I really like you and would like to have had you remain entirely out of this mess. I rescued you once, but I'm afraid it would be impossible to do so again. After rescuing you on the beach, I thought for a while that it might be possible to persuade you to join our operation. We could have used someone like you with international connections. You are respectable and no one would question your integrity. However, I'm afraid you are too straight. I don't believe I could trust you."

John did not disagree with him.

Archy continued, "One of our friends hotwired your VW and drove it here last night after we brought you here. You, my friend, are going to meet with an accident. We also had your camera equipment brought from your room. Late tonight, you will drive your car, too fast, down a mountain road and plunge over a precipice into the valley below. I have shown one of my men how to take pictures and he will take a few in the area. Thus, when your body is found, and the roll of film developed, your accidental death while on a photo jaunt will be confirmed. I will be most upset because you were my good friend. The Inspector General will be distraught too. We can both commiserate over your unfortunate death and concur about the inadvisability of civilians, especially foreigners, becoming involved in unauthorized detective work."

John did not mention that he was expected at Antonio's house at noon. He hoped Antonio would initiate a search for him when he didn't show up. "Are you the head of the smuggling operations?" questioned John.

"I guess I can safely satisfy your curiosity," allowed Archy. "It won't do you any good or us any harm. Senor Martinez finances our operations in this part of the country. He also makes arrangements with brokers in the United States, Canada, South America, and on the continent to sell the merchandise to museums and private collectors."

"Are you saying that these articles, from the Canary Islands, are in demand all over the world? I wouldn't think that some countries, South America for example, would understand or appreciate cultural artifacts from here. It seems incredible!"

"Oh, the artifacts are not only from here. Our network extends almost everywhere. Let me give you an interesting example. In the basement of a temple in mainland China several hundred ancient, hand woven, wedding baskets were discovered by one of our agents. These had beautiful, complex symbolic designs, woven into them. The openwork designs on the outside covered a layer of hand woven, hand dyed cloth, which, in turn, covered another intricate woven design on the inside of each basket. As you can imagine, these handsome baskets would be expected to bring quite a price from collectors. They were only gathering dust where they were. In a sense, we are doing the world a favor by revealing some beautiful objects that would not otherwise ever be seen. At any rate, a member of our organization found a way to remove these baskets without causing too much of a stir. The baskets sold for a great deal of money to a museum in Rome, a collector in Sao Paulo, and an expensive art shop in New York. Senor Martinez himself is a well know collector of oil paintings and antique glass."

"Why are you involved in this, Archy? You obviously earned a lot of respect in your former investigative capacity with the British government."

"Yes, well I never got rich being respectable either. I just didn't fancy spending the rest of my years trying to get by on my miserably low government pension. Besides, I have always enjoyed adventure."

"What about your wife? How does she feel about you being involved in criminal activities?"

"If you are trying to make me feel repentant, forget it, John. This is strictly a business as far as we are both concerned. Now that I have helped break the case for the Inspector General by revealing some of the smugglers, and my cover here in the Canary Islands is blown, as you Americans say, I shan't be much use to the Spanish government. Indeed, my wife and I will probably return to Great Britain. I shall most likely remain in retirement there for a while until the organization convinces some other government, concerned because they are losing too many of their valuables, to hire me. My reputation here will make my chance of being hired elsewhere greater."

"Aren't you afraid some of the captured smugglers will give you away as a double agent?"

"Not really. They are aware that we have good lawyers that will get them light sentences, and that we will take care of their families if they do have to serve prison sentences. They know that when they come out they will have money waiting for them and can expect to live a good life on that. Besides, if one of them did point the finger at me, he wouldn't be believed anyway. There are too many respected people in the community to attest to my good reputation."

"What about Senor Martinez? Based on the pictures I gave the Inspector General of Senor Martinez escorting Maria on board the ocean liner and her subsequent death, he is going to suspect him of involvement in Maria's death and probably in the entire smuggling operation."

"Have no fear. If he does begin to think of him as a possible suspect in the complicity, I shall do everything I can to quiet his fears. Senor Martinez wields a lot of power in the Islands. He is a benefactor to many of the poor people and the small politicians here. As you say in America, he is like motherhood and apple pie. I don't think even the Inspector General would care to fool with him without a great deal of proof. I am going to see that he doesn't get this."

"Tell me one more thing," persisted John, "Was it you who entered the Guanche cave and erased most of the prints and other evidence?"

"Yes, I was only sorry that this hadn't been done before you discovered the body. That was carelessness on my part. I didn't dream anyone would discover the body so soon."

"Did you kill Wayne?"

"No, as a matter of fact, I didn't. Captain Lopez and two of the men who are now in jail did the actual killing."

"Isn't Captain Lopez likely to talk rather than suffer the penalty for murder?"

"It is probable that the Inspector General may have enough clues to link him to Wayne's murder and bring an indictment against him, thanks to you. The pictures you took of the footprints in the cave and the items you found on Captain Lopez' boat, which belonged to Morrison, will most assuredly make him a prime suspect. However, that problem has been taken care of. Plans have already been made to help Captain Lopez escape from jail. We haven't decided yet if we should really allow him to escape or provide for a guard to shoot him when he tries to escape. It would be safer to kill him."

"Why was Wayne killed? Was he a part of the smuggling operation?"

"Yes, he handled distribution of the smaller articles for the organization. He helped us by including stolen items along with his legitimate shipments to the United States. For example, fine lace work is still created in many of the villages in the Islands. A man in Santa Cruz makes a business of contracting for the lace articles to be made. Wayne, in turn, exports them to Europe where they are distributed to exclusive shops."

"This is a legitimate business and brings in a great deal of profit for him. Last month we removed a number of beautiful pieces from the warehouse of the man from Santa Cruz. Wayne was able to include them in one of his regular shipments the very next day. This was before the theft was even discovered. Wayne was also able to serve our cause by being responsible for receiving the larger crated objects when they arrived in the States. He would have them picked up in his company truck, relabel them, and ship them on to a destination specified by us.

Our process is so complex that it would be almost impossible to trace any item from its source to its destination. Unfortunately, Wayne became too greedy and wanted too great a share of the profits. He was good at what he did, but we were forced to dispense with his services."

"Incidentally, we already have a replacement for Wayne - an elderly gentleman who runs a fine antique shop in Puerto de la Cruz. He was the one who searched your room, looking for the film."

"What about Mrs. Schumacher? Was she Wayne's mother? Were you responsible for her murder too?"

"No, she wasn't Wayne's mother. She was well paid to pose as his mother and live in his apartment. She received incoming messages and redirected them to their final destination. Wayne only lived there part of the time. Most of his time was spent traveling. She of course, served as his housekeeper. When Wayne's death was reported to one of our contacts in New York, he made the decision to eliminate Wayne's home and business addresses as quickly as possible. He was afraid that the police in this country and in the United States might decide to cooperate on an investigation into Wayne's death."

"What about Maria? Why was she killed? Did she know too many of your operators in the United States?"

"No, actually, Maria was not from the U.S. She was Spanish, a runaway from a wealthy family. She learned her English from an American governess who practically raised her. She got into the organization in Europe when she met Senor Martinez, who took her under his wing. She was having second thoughts about moral values and had disclosed that she was going to leave the organization. I think you may have influenced her there. Senor Martinez was concerned that she might not be discreet - you know how emotional young people can be. Her death was not a bad one. She knew the young man who killed her. She probably welcomed him coming to her cabin to say goodbye."

"Your death will not be harsh either. I will give you something to relax you before we do the job. I've got to leave now. My wife will send you down some food shortly. Don't get any idea about escaping. If you do, you might have to die a most horrible and painful death with the two guards I have posted upstairs. At least my plans for you include a painless death. I will see you again later. Goodbye!"

With that, Archy untied John's hands and feet and left. John was alone. As promised, an ugly looking character brought down a breakfast tray. Everything on the tray looked appetizing and he was hungry. The thought crossed his mind that perhaps the food was drugged. Probably though, they would wait until the evening meal to drug him. He decided to chance it and ate the meal. When he didn't become drowsy, he knew he had made a good decision.

Now John could concentrate on finding a way to escape. Always an optimist, he explored every inch of the cellar. He collected several broken and jagged bottle parts. These could serve as weapons against the person or persons who arrived to take him to his death. He knew he was not going to die without a struggle.

Sometimes he sat and contemplated his surroundings and the succession of events which led to his present situation. It

all seemed unreal somehow, like scenes from a television drama
or a chapter from a Maigret mystery.

At noon his guard again visited. He left another well
cooked meal but did not say anything. This time John found it
difficult to eat. Probably he was not hungry because of his
morning inactivity. He had not yet burned up his breakfast
calories. Also, he had to admit to himself that he was a little
tense about the situation he was in.

He wondered what kind of pictures Archy's friend was
taking with his camera. John felt sure the Inspector General
would be able to see the difference between the photographs he
had taken earlier and those that might be found in his camera
after his death.

The afternoon passed slowly. Even though John was free
to roam the cellar, he discovered no means of escape from his
dank prison. A third meal was brought at nine in the evening. He
did not plan to eat any of this meal. Even if he had not been
concerned that this meal would be drugged, he was too keyed up
to eat. He had honed his pieces of broken glass to fine edges
using corner stones on the walls of the basement. These weapons
were secreted away on his person. He only hoped he would have
an opportunity to use them at the right time. He could not help
worrying, but he knew he was going to make a good attempt to
save his own life.

By now, Antonio would have known for some time that
he had not arrived at his house for lunch as planned. Had he been
concerned about this? Had he called his room at the hotel and
found him gone? Had he contacted the Inspector General? He
imagined they were investigating his disappearance. Or could
Archy have informed them that he was somewhere taking

pictures? Surely Antonio would not believe that he would not show up for dinner without calling to give him a reason. He hoped they had started a search for him.

John thought it would be a good idea to dispose of some of his meal in case his guards had expected him to consume some kind of drug in it. To this end, he scooped part of the contents of the tray into a corner of the cellar, under one of the wine shelves.

At about ten o'clock the door opened above, his guards came down, and then led him up the stairs. He feigned an unconcerned drowsiness. They seemed to expect this. Each took one of his arms and assisted him up the stairs. They didn't bother to tie his wrists or his legs. One of the men climbed into John's car and John was taken to another car. He was pushed into the back seat where another thug was already seated. His guard then settled himself into the driver's seat and the two cars proceeded slowly down the road. John viewed the scene through half closed eyes. He hung his head forward as if in a drugged state. He saw no sign of Archy. Perhaps he would meet him later at his destination.

Before the cars had gone more than 1000 yards, there appeared to be another car blocking the way. The VW stopped, and the car John was in came to a halt behind. He saw the driver of the VW get out, leaving his lights on. He approached the impeding vehicle.

Suddenly, bright lights were flashed into the back seat blinding John and the man beside him. Simultaneously, the driver of John's car received the same treatment. All the doors of the car were pulled open, and John's captors found themselves with guns pointing directly at their heads. They didn't have time to reach for their own weapons.

The men were ordered from the car. Then the Inspector General leaned down, peered in at John, and gave him a tight grin. "I apologize for not getting to you sooner. We thought it risky to attempt to rescue you when we didn't know exactly the circumstances under which they were holding you. We took Archy into custody this afternoon and forced him to disclose his plans for you. He told us that these men were going to bring you to an overlook point tonight and he was to be there to meet them. They were planning to place you in the VW and push it off the road into a ravine."

"But how did you know where I was?"

"We assigned two of our men to keep an eye on you when you left the station yesterday. One of them was stationed in the hotel room next to yours and had placed a sensitive microphone under the connecting door to your room. These arrangements were made while you were eating. It was but a few minutes after this surveillance system was completely set up that the two thugs were detected entering your room. They followed you out here. One of the men got back to us only after they had assured themselves you were probably going to remain here for a while. It was evident to them that you would not likely be harmed while you were in Archy's home.

"Did Antonio inform you that I did not come to lunch at his house as expected?"

"Yes indeed, he and Guillermo are most agitated. They spent all afternoon insisting that we stage an immediate rescue operation. If you had been harmed, my job would not have been worth a farthing."

"Were you surprised to find out that Archy was a member of the gang?"

"Quite frankly, yes. Since the man who was keeping an eye on you reported his findings, we have done a complete check on him. He does not appear to have any previous record. When we presented our new evidence to the other smugglers we have in jail, however, several of them began to talk, including Captain Lopez. They didn't want to take more than their share of the blame, so they confirmed Archy's part in the caper.

Subsequently, Archy confessed, and we have his statement. It was he that suggested we pick you up when your guards were bringing you to the place where they planned to dispose of you."

"Where did you arrest Archy?"

"After our men had alerted us to where you had been taken, we assigned one of them to keep track of Archy. The other one remained close to Archy's house in case you needed help. Archy left his house in the afternoon and drove to the office of Senor Martinez. He was apparently going to apprise him of the latest development with respect to you. Our man, who had followed him, reported where he was. By this time we had had a chance to develop the film you had taken of Senor Martinez and Maria boarding his ship yesterday afternoon. The pictures were excellent and definitely implicate Martinez with respect to Maria. Although they will not prove that Martinez was responsible for her death, they, along with the fact that Martinez has been dealing with Archy, should strengthen our case against both of them. Only a few hours have passed since we arrested them both, and already Senor Martinez' lawyers are giving us a difficult time, but I suspect we will have enough evidence against them to assure long prison sentences. I also suspect that a number of other persons will tell us what they know, especially if they find themselves accused of being involved in either Maria's or Wayne's death."

The Inspector General helped John out of the car and they drove back to Santa Cruz in a police car. He informed John that the second set of prints had arrived. The pictures of Wayne's shoes, and many of the footprints John had photographed in the storage cave, would serve as excellent corroborating court evidence. He asked that John record another statement and informed him that he would then be free to continue his work in Santa Cruz.

"What about the rest of the international smuggling ring?" asked John.

"The evidence your wife procured in New York has been followed up by the police there. Mr. Morrison's answering service cooperated completely and they were able to provide the police with several other phone numbers and the warehouse location."

"These phone numbers led to the arrest of five more men. Lists were found at the locations where these men were picked up. These lists contained the names of other individuals, all over the United States and Canada, who were involved in the operation. These people are now being investigated by authorities in those areas."

"Have they discovered who murdered Mrs. Schumacher?"

"I have not heard yet. The authorities in the United States will be in touch with me tomorrow. Perhaps we will know something more then. They may never, of course, discover who murdered her. It does appear, though, that the distribution system for delivering stolen goods will be broken up"

"What about the operations in South America and Europe?"

"I understand from our friends in the U.S. that they have a number of leads for the police in South America. They are eager to follow these up. As for Europe, Interpol, I'm sure, will be using the information we have forwarded to them to conduct a massive clean-up operation."

John sat back and relaxed for the duration of the drive to headquarters. He thought about how lucky he was to be alive. He also decided he was going to bring Irene to Santa Cruz. He knew she would enjoy the festivities at Candelaria which were going to take place the following weekend. They would be celebrating the return of the Virgin of Candelaria.

Marilyn Joyce Lafferty Sietsema

ABOUT THE AUTHOR

Known as mom to her three sons, and opa or grandma to her five grandchildren, Marilyn Sietsema was born Marilyn Joyce Lafferty on November 18, 1925, in the small town of Benton, Illinois. It was located in the southern reaches of the state, which has more in common with the South than the North. Her father Nelson Edwin Lafferty, who liked to be called Ned, was a traveling salesman of typewriters and later of roofing materials, and at one point was said to be the fastest typist in Illinois. Her mother, nee Eleanor Mackenzie, was a housewife who'd grown up in Sault Ste. Marie, Ontario.

It wasn't long before Marilyn's family – she was an only child – relocated to the South Side of Chicago, living in a frame tenement at 63rd Street and Stony Island Avenue. The region has long since been rehabbed, and if you visit that corner now, you'll find a public park and landscaped roadways. She used to tell many stories from that time, including one about an older Italian girlfriend who was gunned down by a jealous boyfriend as she watched. It was apparently tough times on the South Side of Chicago, especially as the Great Depression set in.

While Marilyn grew up among Irish and Italians, Marilyn's future husband, Jacob William Sietsema, Jr. lived in a Dutch neighborhood not far away known as Roseland. His father was a math teacher in the Chicago public schools, and he used to recount how in the early 1930s when city paychecks ran months behind, they mainly ate rutabagas, leading to a lifelong hatred of turnips. Marilyn must have eaten plenty of rutabagas, too, and sometimes, when she was much older and more successful in life, used to recite a rhyme that the kids in the street would chant, "The Irish and the Dutch, they never amount to much."

She met Jay after he returned to Chicago from World War II and resumed his education at the University of Chicago, where they both were scholarship students. According to Marilyn, they met in the Balance Room of the Physics Department, which was her major, while Jay studied Chemistry. For a time, Marilyn worked in the lab of Enrico Fermi, who built the world's first nuclear reactor under the stands at the football stadium. On cold days she used to study near the reactor with her cat Blackie, because it was warm there. Jay and Marilyn were later married on April 18, 1947, at the Rockefeller Memorial Chapel on the University of Chicago campus.

After they graduated, they moved to East Lansing, Michigan, where Jay studied for an MS degree in Chemical

Engineering at Michigan State University, with additional coursework at University of Illinois at Champagne-Urbana. His eyesight was thought to be failing, and he decided to take up high school teaching as a profession. So, the couple moved to St. Joseph, Michigan, where their first son Robert was born in 1951. Now it was Marilyn's turn to suffer from poor health, and their son was packed off to stay with his maternal grandparents for a year or so in Chicago while she recovered.

Eventually, they moved back to Chicago and Jay got a job at International Minerals and Chemicals, where he was instrumental in formulating the monosodium glutamate brand Ac'cent. The threesome was living in the idyllic town of Northbrook, then almost more rural than suburban, when twins David and William were born in 1955. She became an avid member of the Twins Club in Northbrook, pushing a double stroller around town, and the family became members of the Village Presbyterian Church.

Around 1959, Jay, Marilyn, and offspring moved to Minneapolis, where Jay took a job as a formulator of food products at Pillsbury. Marilyn continued to raise the boys, but soon had a hankering to start a career. She took a job as a librarian at the Breck School, a fancy private school in Minneapolis, as the family lived in the western suburb of Golden Valley. It was then a suburb of modest, newly built frame houses on lots denuded of everything but a few saplings. For the boys it was heaven, as they played on vacant lots and in a nearby creek full of snakes and frogs.

Eventually, the family moved to the tonier and more established suburb of Edina to the south, though into a neighborhood that was another suburban frontier, in what was then the modern equivalent of homesteading. All the boys rode their bikes through still-farmed neighborhoods, and Robert worked summers as a caddie in a golf course as the twins collected crayfish from a nearby stream.

In 1967, Jay accepted a new job in Dallas working as a snack-foods formulator for Frito-Lay, which had recently been acquired by Pepsico. They settled in a North Dallas neighborhood, and Marilyn resumed her education, taking a PhD from Texas Woman's University in Early Childhood Education. She taught at TWU, and later snagged a job directing a new daycare center in Flower Mound, Texas, where she was able to apply the principles she'd learned as an academic to create a modern and progressive childcare institution.

And Marilyn loved being with kids again, as hers had gone away to college. Eventually, her kids had kids, and she was a doting grandmother to Carrie and David Sietsema, David's children; Jessica and Laura Sietsema, Bill's children; and Tracy Jane Van Dyk, Robert's daughter. Jay and Marilyn eventually retired, and moved to Sun City in Georgetown, Texas, where they had a house in the retirement community, but eventually moved to more compact apartments, first in Pflugerville and later in southwest Austin.

Jay died September 7, 2018, and Marilyn lived for three more years, passing away on October 2, 2021. They are survived by her three children, five grandchildren, and three great grandchildren – Lance and Tate Gundrum, and Tracy Stella Van Dyk.

Marilyn was interred on October 27, 2021, at Fort Sam Houston National Cemetery in San Antonio, Texas. The grave for Jacob and Marilyn Sietsema is located in Section 115, Site 45.

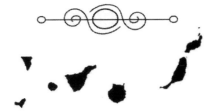

Printed in Great Britain
by Amazon